Nothing Here but
S T O N E S

Nothing Here but
STONES

Nancy Oswald

Filter Press, LLC
Palmer Lake, Colorado

Library of Congress Cataloging-in-Publication Data

Oswald, Nancy.
  Nothing here but stones / Nancy Oswald.
      pages cm
  Previously published in 2004 by Henry Holt.
  Summary: In 1882, ten-year-old Emma and her family, along with other
Russian Jewish immigrants, arrive in Cotopaxi, Colorado, where they face
inhospitable conditions as they attempt to start an agricultural colony, and lonely
Emma is comforted by the horse whose life she saved.
  ISBN 978-0-86541-150-0 (pbk. : alk. paper)
  1. Jews--Colorado--Juvenile fiction. [1. Jews--United States--Fiction. 2.
Frontier and pioneer life--Colorado--Fiction. 3. Immigrants--Fiction. 4. Russian
Americans--Fiction. 5. Colorado--History--1876-1950--Fiction.] I. Title.
  PZ7.O865No 2013
  [Fic]--dc23
                         2012050099

Cover Design by Daniel R. Pratt, Pratt Brothers Composition, LLC
Cover copyright ©2013 by Filter Press, LLC
Interior layout by Kooima Kreations

Filter Press, LLC
Palmer Lake, Colorado

Printed in the United States of America

Dedication

Dedicated to the descendants of
the Cotapaxi Jewish Colony
(1882-1884)

And
to the memory of my Mom,
Wanda D. Taylor

1

The loose thread on Papa's suit is getting longer. I've been trying hard to ignore it, but when I look at Papa's back, it waves at me like a tiny black worm. I want to reach out and pull it, but I'm afraid his coat will unravel like the threads of our lives, and there will be nothing left. If Mama were here, she would use a needle to weave that thread back into the fabric of the suit, and it would look just like new.

When Papa sleeps, the thread disappears. It slides below the top of the seat as he scoots down to get more comfortable … usually at night when the only sound is the groaning of the cars and the clattering of the wheels on the track.

And the snoring. From all over the train, but especially from Etta Stokes. She sounds like Mrs. Washer's cow when it got loose and ran through the streets of Kishinev, right into the middle of the Tsar's soldiers. It happened so fast, all I remember is the sound of the shot, a loud bellow, and blood on the cobbled street. Mrs. Washer screamed and started to argue, but one of the soldiers pulled out his whip and struck her.

"Stinking Jew," he said.

Papa's face turned to ashes when I told him. He looked slowly around our house, gazing first at Mama's sewing basket and ending with a long, quiet stare at the bookcase near the table where he taught his Hebrew students. Soon after that, we began to pack.

Except for the snoring, I like nighttime on the train best. Ruth curls up like a cat with her head on my lap, and after she goes to sleep I press my face to the window and look up at the glittery stars, imagining that one of them is Mama looking down from heaven to make sure we're all well.

Papa says it's not good to dwell on the dead. I try not to, but when Mama died, it left a hole bigger than the black night sky.

Little Leb is awake. Adar is looking back at me. Soon she will say, "Emma, it's your turn to hold your brother."

I don't want to. I really don't want to. My arms hurt, and my legs are tired. I have been bouncing Leb all the way from New York ... for almost five days. But I can't say no to Adar. She will complain to Papa that I am not helping, and he will look at me over the rims of his glasses and raise up his eyebrows in a way that says, *What child of mine could be so willful?*

It's not that I am unwilling, but Adar gives me the baby every time he is awake. Those are the times he is squirming to be let down, and I have to bounce and play with him to keep him from crying. If he gets noisy, Etta frowns at me from across the aisle, and everyone else pretends they cannot hear. I can tell by watching Papa when it is bothering him. The back of his suit stretches tightly across his shoulders, and the little black thread stands up straight.

Papa says I shouldn't feel sorry for myself. "Look around you at all the other people. They have traveled just as far. You don't hear them complaining."

When I look around the crowded car, I know why they do not complain. They are too tired of traveling. Like me, they are ready to be off the train.

Mochel Kahn has just changed his seat. I think Adar is trying to impress him by cooing and smiling at little Leb. Adar cried when we left home. "Who will be my matchmaker in America?" she sobbed. She is sixteen, and I think she has time, but the worst thing she can imagine is dying an old maid.

"Wait until you are my age," Adar said to me one day on our long journey across the Atlantic Ocean. "You will worry, too."

It is hard to imagine what things will be like in five more years. I can't even imagine ten minutes from now. From moment to moment, out the window of the train, things are changing. At first I thought everything in America would look like New York City, with shops and crowded streets, but I have discovered, the farther west we travel, that there are long stretches of nothing. Absolutely nothing. Places as flat as matzo.

I only hope the place we are going to is not so empty. Papa says it is land for farming. We will grow crops and own land. He says we are lucky because it is something we could not do in Russia. The Tsar would not allow it.

I think we will need more than luck. Before we left New York, I overheard Papa tell Benjamin Stokes that most of our money was spent to pay for the trip across the Atlantic and our expenses in New York City. The rest of the money has been sent

3

ahead to Mr. Reis, who will have houses and equipment ready for us when we arrive in Cotopaxi.

Co-toe-pax-ee. The word hurts my ears. I can't get used to the English language—it sounds so sharp and stiff. I wish people here spoke Yiddish; it's much more like music.

Papa says we will have to learn to speak like Americans, but when I listen to Mr. Stokes translate for us, I think he does not like it either. His words sound like an ax chopping wood into kindling.

"Where … is … the … train … to … Co- toe-pax-ee?"

This is what he said to the ticket salesman at the station in Pueblo. The man leaned forward and squinted between the bars of his cage. His eyes grew as round as kiddush cups when he saw all of us standing there.

"Cotopaxi?" the man said, bending one ear sideways as if he could not believe what he heard.

Benjamin nodded, holding up our tickets. The man walked slowly out of his cage to the door of the station. He pointed to a set of tracks that faded away like little stitches on a quilt.

"Good luck," the man said, shaking his head as he returned to his work.

"Mazel tov," Mr. Stokes answered. He started toward the train, and everyone followed in a line. We were last: Papa, Ruth, Adar with little Leb, and me, like a caboose, at the end.

Mazel tov. Mazel tov. Mazel tov-mazel tov-mazeltov-mazeltov-mazeltov-mazeltov. The sound of wheels on the tracks made my eyelids heavy, and after closing them, I did not remember anything until Ruth pulled on my sleeve.

4

"Emma, the rocks are taller than the buildings in New York City!" I opened my eyes to see a crystal blue river shadowed by red rock walls that blocked the sun as the train crawled along the track.

I wanted to see the full height of the cliffs, so I opened the window and stretched out, twisting so I could look up. I felt a tug on the back of my dress.

You're going to fall out." Adar yanked at me with her right hand, still holding little Leb with her left. A hot cinder flicked my cheek and I ducked back inside, hating the way Adar treats me ... always bossing ... always like a child.

"The rocks are like a giant's mouth. It's going to swallow us up!" Ruth said.

The taller the rocks, the slower we crept, inch by inch, *cachug, cachug.*

Adar buried her face in little Leb's neck, and I heard her say a quiet prayer.

For a few moments, the train stopped. We hung over the rapids with only the rails and a few timbers separating us from the water that rushed between the red rock walls.

Ruth squeezed my hand, and all through the car people began to talk nervously and point.

Benjamin Stokes wobbled unsteadily to the front of the car and stuttered his English words to the conductor. The conductor smiled at him and patted his shoulder, then Mr. Stokes turned and spoke in Yiddish to Hannah and Sophie Shorr as they clung to each other near the center aisle, their faces white as the foam on the rapids.

Papa sat stiffly next to Adar, his shoulders squared and flat. The little thread on the back of his suit held its breath.

At long last I heard a hiss of steam coming from the engine of the train. First it came in long, slow gasps, then in short little breaths that finally heaved into a steady rhythm as the train picked up speed.

Adar stopped praying and opened her eyes; Hannah and Sophie scooted back to the window; the little thread on the back of Papa's suit began to jiggle up and down once more. I did not realize that I had been holding my breath, too, and like the train, I exhaled and started to move again.

I looked backward over my shoulder to see the hanging track where we had just been. The rocks closed in behind us like a large door shutting. Then I looked forward, toward the place we were going—the place that would be our new home. There was no turning back.

Adar handed Leb to me, and the angel of sleep must have been hovering over him. He leaned against my shoulder, and his eyelids drooped. Ruth, too, managed to curl herself into a ball and squeeze her head onto my lap. The car was quiet now, and I wondered if everyone was looking out the window, like me, and thinking, *How will we eat all these rocks?* I wonder if, like me, they were wanting to go home.

"When we are in America," Papa had told me, "we will be safe from the Tsar's soldiers. In America we can own land. In America they cannot tell you where you must live, and they cannot put you in the army for twenty-five years because you are Jewish."

The grass near the tracks leaned over, gray and thin, making me think of Grandma Rose when she said good-bye. "Why won't you come with us?" I asked her.

"I am too old to change," she said. "My people are here. My things are here. My heart is here."

My heart is there, too.

The train whistle will not let me think anymore. The wheels squeal, and the train slows to a stop.

Give me the baby," Adar says. She stands up, straightens her dress, and reaches over the seat for him. Papa stands, too, taking two bags from the rack above his head and one from below his seat.

I look at Ruth, not wanting to wake her. Her lips curve into a smile, and she looks like she is dreaming of the sweet cake from the vendor in Denver where we changed trains. He did not even ask us to pay.

"Ruth." I shake her gently. She sits up and rubs the sleep from her eyes, then looks out the window and exclaims, "Why are we stopping? There is nothing here!"

I try to tell her that I have seen a few houses and scattered buildings, but now, from the window of our train, all we can see is a single building with a wide front porch. From the roof hangs a wooden sign with an American word, which Papa says must be read backward, from left to right, in a way that hurts my eyes.

"This can't be it," Ruth says, with her nose still pressed to the window. I pull her away, and by the time I get our bundle from under the seat, the train car is as empty as a synagogue on Sunday.

I hurry to get off the train, bumping the bundle between the seats and pulling Ruth down the aisle. When I turn the corner to go down the steep steps, the rope of my bundle snags on the handrail, pulling it backward. I fly forward off the bottom step, landing on the rocky ground beside the track. Ruth follows, landing on top of me. Behind us comes the bundle, and a shower of our belongings.

I stand slowly, pulling Ruth up by the elbow and dusting off my dress. It is then that I look at the group of people gathered on the platform. A man wearing a vest and torn shirt points at me and says something in English. The people near him laugh. He loops his thumbs into his belt, and there I see two guns dangling near his fingertips.

Suddenly, I think of Mrs. Washer's cow, and the Tsar's soldier saying, "Stinking Jew."

I kneel to pick up our things: the embroidered covers for challah bread and matzo, kiddush cups and candlesticks, Papa's prayer shawl, and our best white tablecloth.

It is not even a minute later when the whistle blows again. The train pulls away, and I watch the conductor wave from the caboose and vanish inside. As he closes the door, I look down at the track. On the ground near my feet are Mama's prayer book and a picture of her in her wedding dress. The picture lies in two pieces, sliced in half by the wheels of the departing train.

I pick up the pieces of Mama, the things from the broken bundle, grab Ruth by the hand, and follow Papa and the others to the waiting wagons.

2

We have, I am sure, the smallest room in the hotel. It is worse than our small space on the boat when we crossed the Atlantic. When Papa told me I would have to share a bed with Etta Stokes, I could not hide my disappointment. "It is the snoring," I told him. "My ears will fall off!"

Papa frowned at me, and I knew I should not have complained.

"You should be thankful to have a bed," Adar snapped. "The hotel is full, and many are sleeping on the floor."

It was Ruth who saved me. "Look, Papa," she said. "Little Leb can fit in here."

She pulled out the bottom drawer from a large dresser and showed Papa how a blanket could be folded inside to make a crib. "Emma can share the bed with Adar and me."

Papa thought about this for a moment, then smiled and patted Ruth's head. "It will make Benjamin happy to have a place in bed with his wife," he said.

Papa rolled out his own blankets on the floor near the door and left for a meeting.

"We are only here for one day," Adar said. "You should not have spoken to Papa that way."

"You are not the one to have a windstorm in your ear," I said, and then my face grew hot as Etta came into the room with her luggage and placed it on the second bed that was pushed up against the wall.

Adar sat down on the edge of our bed and rubbed the sides of her temples with both hands. "My head feels like it has a large hammer inside."

I knew what was coming, and before she asked, I went to get her a wet cloth to lay across her forehead. It was on the way back that I heard an angry voice coming from the dining room of the hotel. It was Papa's. "I do not understand why our houses are not finished. We sent the money so they could be built." He paused for a moment, then added, "And not enough houses. We have more families coming."

"I have just spoken with Mr. Reis," Mr. Stokes said. "The money has been spent, and there is nothing we can do about it."

"Everything should have been ready for our arrival." Papa raised his voice. The other men grumbled in agreement. "We have no money to stay in the hotel."

"Mr. Reis said he will do what he can to help us."

I listened a little longer, thinking this news would make Adar's headache as large as Solomon's house. The last thing I heard Papa say as I tiptoed down the hall was "Tomorrow we will go to see the houses. We will do what we need to finish them."

By the time I returned to the room, the cloth for Adar's head was stiff and drying. "I can get you another," I offered.

10

Never mind. No one cares if I have a headache."

"I care," Ruth said, but Adar did not listen and made me feel like I was the one who made her head hurt.

The next morning when Papa left, I wished for Adar's headache instead of the stomachache that felt like a wet stocking twisting inside me.

I watched Papa cross the river with the other men on a footbridge with fraying ropes. When he got to the other side, he was swallowed up by the rocks, trees, and bushes of a smaller canyon.

I could not get the picture out of my mind: Papa and the other men, carrying hammers, boards, and buckets of nails. The bridge wiggled like a long caterpillar as they crossed, and then they were gone.

"Quit daydreaming and help!" Adar threw a shirt at me, and I unwound it and smoothed it flat on a warm rock at the river's edge.

"What if Papa does not come back?" I asked.

"Don't be silly. He will be back before dark."

"I heard him say it is a long walk to where the houses are."

"You worry too much."

Etta Stokes sat upstream from us, holding little Leb and watching Ruth and her friend Hazel wade out into the shallow part of the river to wash themselves. I could hear them squeal as they squatted down into the water and sprang up again, trying to see who could stay in the cold water the longest. Etta tossed them a bar of soap.

"I do not know why Mrs. Baker will not let us use the tub

and wringer at the hotel," I said. "She is not using it."

Adar rubbed a pair of Papa's pants on a rock that jutted up near our washing hole. Water trickled from there into a second pool, where she swished the pants for rinsing. "There are too many of us," Adar said. "And too many clothes."

I looked at the pile on the shore, thinking, *We will still be scrubbing at midnight.* Just then I heard a scream, and Etta ran into the river, holding up her dress. She reached down and yanked Leb up by the arm, pulling him from the water before he went under.

"*Gevalt!*" Adar dropped Papa's pants and ran. I bounded after her, arriving just as Etta staggered out of the water, skirt soaked and dragging.

Now Leb was wailing, and Etta, white as a sheet, handed him to Adar. "I only put him down for a moment. I did not think he would go into the water."

Adar stripped off Leb's wet clothes, and I hurried to the pile of unwashed clothes and grabbed one of Papa's shirts to wrap him in. When I got back, Ruth and Hazel were standing naked on the shore like two plucked hens.

"What happened?" Ruth asked. She peeked under Papa's shirt to make sure Leb was all right.

"It is Leb," Adar said. "He can no longer be trusted to stay in one place."

"I will say one hundred prayers of gratefulness that he did not drown," Etta said. "Come, girls. Your bath is finished." Etta shooed Ruth and Hazel toward their clothes, took Leb from Adar, and marched up the trail to the hotel.

"How could you have been so careless?" Adar said as we tramped back down the shoreline. "I'll have to watch him myself from now on."

I did not know why I was getting blamed, and I was about to say so when I looked at the water hole where Adar had been scrubbing clothes. "Papa's pants!" I cried, pointing. "They are floating away."

We looked down the river in time to see one leg of the pants snag on a piece of driftwood, bob a couple of times, then sink and be forever gone.

Adar sat down and held her head in her hands, and I was afraid another headache would start. I told her, "Better to lose Papa's pants than little Leb."

"Better to lose nothing at all."

Adar sighed and took a skirt from the laundry pile, swishing it in the washing hole. After she scrubbed and rinsed it, she handed it to me for wringing and hanging. I draped it over a low bush, then turned back for the blouse Adar had rinsed.

All afternoon, I waited for Papa, turning and folding clothes as they dried. After supper, we brought the remaining laundry back to the hotel. I walked down one last time, to watch for Papa coming across the wobbly bridge.

Later, I sat on the porch of the hotel in a wicker chair, waiting. I waited until the black night sky flickered with stars, and I could no longer see the river. Once I thought I heard footsteps and the sound of a branch snapping, but it was only Mrs. Baker. She pointed to the remaining oil in the lamp and frowned, taking the light away.

I sat and waited some more in the dark, listening to the creek that trickled past our hotel. Beyond that, I heard the river rushing and singing, *Papa, where are you, where are you, where are you?*

Papa did not answer, and so I finally entered the hotel and found our room in the dark.

"Where have you been?" Adar whispered as I climbed into bed.

"Waiting for Papa," I told her.

Adar groaned and rolled over, wrapping the blanket around her and tucking it underneath, leaving Ruth and me the leftovers. I tugged some in my direction, and Adar tugged back until Ruth was squeezed between us like fruit in a strudel.

I tried to sleep, but Etta's breathing sounded like a great wind sucking in trees and rocks and blowing them out again. For some reason, it made me think of sitting in the synagogue with Mama, just the two of us, when she told me the story of God bringing forth the plants and the trees, the wild and tame beasts, and all living creatures. "And then he blew life into them with a great force ..."

Finally, our door creaked open. Papa and Benjamin came in, and I heard the quiet thump of Papa's boots as he placed them beside his sleeping mat.

I waited for Papa to come over and pat Ruth's head and give Leb a kiss, the way he always does, but I only heard a rustling sound and the quiet whisper of Papa's prayers. They were drowned by the roar of Etta's snoring.

3

"Make yourself useful," Etta says to me. "Too many frowns pull the sun from the sky."

I am trying to smile, but every day that passes makes it more difficult. I think I have caught a disease from Mrs. Baker. When we first came here, eight days ago, she smiled and brought us everything we needed. Now she goes about the day looking busy all the time. When someone asks her for something, she shrugs and acts as if she does not understand.

Just this morning, I heard her say the word "Jew" to Mrs. Young, the cook, and I could tell by her voice it was not meant to be kind. Mrs. Young laughed and waved her away, then bent down to give little Leb a cookie. Leb is the only one that does not have to worry about learning to speak English. He just smiles and points with his pudgy fingers, and everyone jumps to please him.

Even Adar is at his mercy, and she does not usually like anyone telling her what to do.

"I am taking Leb to the room for a nap," Adar said to me after we had finished our noon meal. "Make sure you do not get lost."

Lost! I thought. *Where would I go?* "You are treating me like a baby," I said.

"If that is true, I would be making you lie down for a rest like little Leb." She took him down the hall to our room.

With nothing else to do, I went outside to the porch of the hotel and leaned over the railing. From where I stood, I could see the bridge across the river and the trail through the low bushes to the place where we washed our clothes. If I turned and looked to my right, I could see the creek they called Bernard and to my left, the rocky ridge where the sun comes up beyond Mr. Black's store.

Then there is nothing … the nothing we saw from our train window. Where did Adar think I would go?

It was then I noticed a horse tied to the hitching rail on the side of the hotel. I climbed over the porch rail and slid to the ground, walking over slowly to look at it. As I approached, it swiveled its head to look at me and flicked one ear. Carefully, I reached my hand up and touched the white star on its forehead. To my surprise, it bumped me with its nose, nuzzling me.

A voice behind me spoke. "Hello."

I jumped and turned, feeling like I had been caught taking an extra sweet from a candy jar. A boy, a little taller than I, stood there looking at me. I stepped away from the horse, afraid he would be upset. Instead, he smiled and nodded, touching the rim of the large dusty hat he wore.

I tried to think what to do. To leave, I would have to back away, step by step, along the side of the horse, or move past the boy, who blocked my way. Before I could decide, the horse made a noise that sounded like a wrinkled sneeze and nuzzled me again.

Suddenly I remembered Papa's warning. "Stay away from horses. Especially the ones the Tsar's soldiers ride. You could get trampled to death."

These are American horses, I thought. *They cannot be so bad.*

The boy said something to me in English, and now I could not leave without being rude. He untied the horse and held out the reins to me.

"Would you like to ride?" He patted the saddle and made a motion with his head. He smiled at me again.

From the corner of my eye, I saw Adar hurry down the front steps of the hotel porch. She bustled toward Mr. Black's store, glancing sideways, toward the river, as she went. I followed her gaze. Mochel Kahn was hiking up the trail to the store, carrying a broken shovel.

When I looked back at the horse, the boy was still holding the reins out to me and smiling. I shook my head and spoke to him in Yiddish, waving my hands to try to explain to him that I had never been on a horse before.

He continued to smile, then pointed to himself. "Charlie," he said. "Charlie Young."

This is where Mama would have asked me if my feet were growing roots. It was time to get going! But as much as I wanted my legs to move, my feet stayed planted. The large round eyes of the horse pulled at me, and I did not want to leave its side.

I pointed to myself and said, "Emma. Emma Lisovsky."

"Emma," he repeated.

Suddenly there was a rustling under the porch of the hotel. A moment later, Ruth crawled out from her hiding place and stepped over. She stood beside me and pointed to herself. "Ruth," she said boldly.

Charlie laughed, and repeated Ruth's name. Then he pointed at the horse and spoke in English. "Horse. Mr. Black's horse."

"Horse," Ruth repeated without hesitation. She stepped in front of me, reaching up to stroke the side of its neck.

"Ride?" Charlie asked. He patted the saddle again.

Ruth's eyes sparkled. She wiggled in next to the horse, bumping me out of the way, and tried to lift her foot up into the stirrup. Charlie grabbed her by the waist and swung her into the saddle as if she were no heavier than a rag doll. She grabbed the large leather knob at the front of the seat and perched there proudly like the Tsarina Catherine.

"You must get off," I said sternly to Ruth.

"Horse." Ruth said the word in English, then spoke in Yiddish. "Look at me, Emma! I'm up on a horse!" She smiled brightly.

At that moment Rachel Schloff came out of the hotel and walked to the porch rail with a pile of blankets to be aired. She took one look at Ruth on the horse and dropped her blankets. "Come quickly!" she screamed. "The boy is stealing our Ruth!"

Rachel hurried down the steps of the porch, followed by a flock of women, aprons flapping. They surrounded us, cackling like upset hens.

"Put the girl down," Rachel demanded, hands on her hips.

Charlie's face turned crimson. He glanced around, frightened, looking for a way to escape.

Suddenly Adar appeared, pushing her way into the center of the group. She snatched Ruth from the saddle and plunked her down on the ground. She turned to me and said, "How could you let this happen? Papa is not going to like it when I tell him."

The other women nodded, not noticing Charlie pull the horse away from the group and leave without a backward glance.

"It was Ruth," I said. "She just wanted to sit for a moment."

"Feh!" Etta Stokes spoke. "It isn't proper."

"It is not a thing a girl should be doing," Rachel clucked.

"I have never seen anything like it."

"You should have told Ruth no," Adar said.

"I have seen lots of American women riding—" I stopped as soon as the words were out of my mouth. One by one I looked at the frowning faces around me.

"The girl is ill from the heat," said one.

"The girl forgets who she is."

The women, still grumbling, walked away until just Ruth and I stood gaping at the empty spot where the horse had been.

"And now I will be in trouble with Papa for what you have done," I said to her.

She did not seem to care, but motioned for me to follow her under the porch. "Come see what I have found."

I ducked under, crawling behind Ruth until we came upon a mother cat with four kittens curled together in the soft dirt. I was reaching for one when I heard the thunder of footsteps above us and Adar shouting, "Where is he? Where can he be?"

"The river!" Sarah Luper cried.

"I'll check toward the creek!" said Etta, heading the other way.

From our hiding place, we could see legs and skirts flying in every direction. We hurried out as quickly as we could, bumping smack into Adar, who had leaned down to look under the porch.

"Do you have him? Is he with you?"

"Have who?" asked Ruth.

"Leb! He's gone! Papa will never forgive us if he is lost," Adar said.

We did not lose him, I thought crossly, and then I began to worry, wondering where I should look.

Just then, an excited voice from inside the hotel shouted, "He's here! He's here!"

We rushed inside and found Mrs. Young jiggling Leb on her broad hip. She looked surprised when everyone crowded around her.

"Tateleh, tateleh," Adar said, taking Leb and smothering him with wet, sloppy kisses.

Mrs. Young looked bewildered. She did a pantomime showing us how Leb had toddled into the kitchen and pulled himself up on the chair near where she was rolling out dough for a batch of sugar cookies.

"He can climb now!" Adar kissed him again. "You are getting to be such a big, strong boy."

I almost cried with relief as I gave Leb a kiss of my own and squeezed his bare toes.

"Papa will not need to know about *this*!" Adar gave me a look as sharp as a needle.

I don't know when she thought I would be able to tell him. He has been gone every day from first light until dark, and sometimes all night. It is only on the Sabbath we are sure to see him, and then Papa is too busy. After our prayers, he goes with the other men to talk about when our houses will be finished and where we will find money to buy the things we still need.

Meetings and meetings and more meetings. In New York, Papa had meetings with our landlord to arrange for our stay and meetings with the Hebrew Emigrant Aid Society to decide where we would settle.

One day I complained about all the meetings, and I am sorry I did. Etta Stokes snapped at me. "It's because we have no rabbi, and someone must help with the decisions."

"It is because your papa is a Hebrew teacher. People respect and look up to him," Sarah Luper said.

"It is because your papa needs to stay busy to forget about your mama," Rachel said.

"You complain too much," Adar scolded me. "Papa has always been busy."

This must be true, but when Mama was alive, I did not notice so much. When Mama was alive, I had someone to talk to.

4

I am sitting in Mrs. Baker's rocking chair, doing my best not to move. If I try to leave, the chair will make a loud creaking sound, and I will be caught like a mouse in a trap. Not by Mrs. Baker, who does not allow anyone to sit in her chair, but by Papa and the others, who have not seen me. If I am lucky, they will not look this way, and Papa will not be angry with me for being in a place I should not be and for doing something I should not be doing.

I did not mean to be here, but when I passed the dining-room door, I spied Mrs. Baker's chair in the corner. *Come over,* it said to me. *I am lonely, too.*

I did not think anyone would mind if I sat in it for a minute to see what it was like. I planned to rock a few times and leave, but the chair made music when it tipped back and forth, and I was making a song along with the ticking of the grandfather's clock, which stood behind me on the floor.

If I had left when I first heard the sound of boots on the hotel steps, I might have had time to slip away. Instead, I sit very still and hear everything, which takes twice as long to say because Benjamin has to change the words from Yiddish to English and back again for Mr. Reis. He is the tall man who comes to the hotel asking for Papa and Benjamin—the man we sent our money to, the man who helped to bring us here.

"There is no longer enough money for you to stay in this hotel," Mr. Reis says as he shifts in his chair. "You must leave."

Papa leans forward toward Mr. Reis as he speaks. "Our houses are still without windows or doors."

"I have no more money to pay for your lodging."

"But the money we sent you—"

"The money did not go as far as I thought."

"Please …" Mr. Schloff clasps his hands to his chest and leans forward, almost kneeling at Mr. Reis's feet. "There is much we still need."

"I'm sorry." Mr. Reis stands briskly and places his hat on his head. "The cost for the hotel is too high. I cannot help you any longer."

When Mr. Reis leaves, his footsteps sound like coffin lids banging down. I hold my breath, listening to the *ticktock-ticktock* of the grandfather's clock behind me, afraid the pendulum will stop and freeze in place.

Finally Abraham Overby speaks. "We don't even have a wagon to haul our things."

"In the morning, I will ask Mr. Black if he will loan us one," Benjamin says.

"We have already borrowed so much—"

Just then the rocker creaks backward with a long, low groan. All eyes in the room turn toward me, but I see only Papa's. He

23

frowns at me, and the rocker grows to an enormous size with me, small as a doll, sitting in it.

I do not know how I make my legs move, but I spring from the chair and dash down the hall, bumping into Etta Stokes, who is balancing an arm-load of freshly folded clothes. The clothes topple, blocking the narrow corridor.

"There is a fire in the dining room?" Etta snaps.

I stoop to help Etta pick up and refold the clothes, but she makes me do them twice until they are to her liking. "I have never seen a girl like you," she says. "Help me take these to the room."

Adar does not make things better. She needs a clean wrapper for Leb and cannot find one. "I thought you washed them," she scolds me.

"They were not quite dry, so I hung them on a bush near the creek."

"And you did not bring them in before dark? They will be all damp from the dew."

Quietly I tiptoe back down the hall, past the entrance to the dining room, where the men are still sitting. As I go out the side door of the hotel, I hold the screen door so it will not snap back on its springs. Groping for the bushes with my hands and feeling my way with my feet, I walk like a blind person to the creek.

When I find the bushes, I sit down for a moment, listening to the water burble and an owl *who-whoing* in the distance. I look up at the dome of stars above, and it makes me think of Mama's black woolen shawl that she used to wrap around me.

24

"Mama," I cry. "I did not mean to upset Papa. I only wanted to sit in the rocker. It was nice, Mama. And when I rocked, it felt like a large, warm lap."

A breeze ruffles the bushes that hold Leb's wrappers. I listen, thinking somehow Mama will answer me. Instead I hear the owl and the laughing of the creek. I gather Leb's wrappers and hurry inside.

5

I think there are things more interesting than staring at the swinging tail of a cow. One way, then the other, it waves back and forth like a hairy mop. Unless there is a fly to swat—then it circles around and swishes sideways. If you are not careful, it will swish in your face and you will get a mouthful of dust and tangled cow hair.

I am the one who has the job of walking the cow up the hill to our new house. "Ruth is too little," Papa said. "And Adar will have to carry Leb."

I do not like being in the middle of the family. There is never an excuse. I cannot say I am too old or too young. There is no room to wiggle. Being in the middle means being stuck like the wheel of the wagon that carried our things up the wide sandy draw of Oak Grove Creek. It took six strong men to roll the wagon out, while Charlie, the boy that drove, whipped the horses forward.

At least the cow did not get stuck. If I poked her with a stick on the right hip, she turned to the left, and when I poked her on the left hip, she turned right. For the most part, she plodded along beside the creek, following the wagon and the line of people in front of us.

"I did not know your sister could walk so fast," Etta Stokes said as she hiked up beside me. "I think maybe she is flirting."

I looked ahead of me down the winding creek bed to see Adar with Leb on her hip, struggling to keep up with Mochel Kahn. She did not look like she was flirting, only trying to find someone to help her carry the baby.

"Trouble starts with a small seed and grows like a weed," Sarah Luper said as she joined the conversation.

"Trouble for Mochel, I think," Etta said.

"Trouble for everyone when Mindel and Jonas arrive."

I wanted to ask Etta more about Mindel and Jonas, but already she was saying, "I suppose all we need now is more trouble." She mopped her brow with the tail of her scarf.

"For me, I am glad to trade the trouble of the hotel for the trouble of my own home," Sarah said.

"A home, no. A roof over our heads, yes."

Just then we came to a place where the trail crossed the creek. We had to jump from stone to stone, balancing carefully, to get to the other side. The milk cow splashed across and halted in a patch of green grass on the opposite shore, lowering her head to eat. I hit her hard with my stick to get her moving again, and she kicked up her heels and trotted ahead to show me what she thought of my behavior.

When she settled down again, I looked up and saw the snow-covered peaks of a great mountain range towering above the rocky bluffs along the creek.

"Sangre de Cristo Mountains," Sarah said. "It means 'Blood of Christ.'"

"Perhaps we have been sent to the wrong place." Etta laughed, but her laughter did not seem happy.

The cow stopped to eat again, and by the time I got her going, Etta and Sarah had moved away, and now everyone was ahead of me. Even Ruth, who had only a small bundle to carry, skipped up in front with her friend Hazel.

A cow is not such bad company, I tried to tell myself. I trudged on and passed the time by watching the clouds that drifted above in the clear blue sky and listening to the little birds chirp in the bushes that lined the creek.

Finally we met a road that came down a steep hill and crossed the creek. Papa and the others were gathered there.

"What is taking you so long?" Adar asked. "We have been here forever, waiting."

I wanted to tell her I would trade the cow for little Leb in a minute, but I did not even have time to catch my breath before the wagon started moving again. Everyone picked up their bundles to follow.

"Is this our road?" I asked Papa as he swung up his pack.

Papa shook his head. "It is the road to Salida, a town up the river." I looked in that direction and could see two tracks running over a low hill and disappearing into the trees. Beyond that, the terrain looked dangerous and unsafe.

"Which way do we go?" I asked.

Papa pointed to a narrow trail climbing up away from the creek. I could not believe my eyes. "At the top of that hill on the flat," Papa explained, "there are a few houses. Some of us will stop there." He paused for a moment. "The other houses are farther." He pointed toward the mountain peaks. "Not far from the edge of those trees."

I followed Papa's finger with my eyes and swallowed hard. The Blood of Christ Mountains. Where he pointed made the trail to Salida look tame. We could not possibly be going that far!

The cow did not think so either. It took five of us to push her up the steep trail away from the creek. After that, she kept trying to turn back. I did not blame her. With every step, the land became more rocky and steep.

When we left the first group of houses, I felt suddenly afraid. More than half the people stopped there. After we unloaded their things from the wagon, we continued up the mountain trail, only a small group now. We dipped down into brush-filled ravines and climbed out again with nothing before us but the windswept slopes of the Blood of Christ Mountains.

I shivered, trying to think of warm things like Mama's bread, hot from the oven, and Grandma Rose's quilt, but every time I looked at the snow-covered ridges, I saw gnarly, unwelcoming fingers pointing and warning us to stay away.

"How are we going to farm up here?" I heard Etta ask Sarah. Now they were behind me, breathing hard and talking less. Even the cow seemed too tired to do anything but stumble up the rocky path.

"I see the houses!" Ruth shouted.

Above the cow's bony back, where the mountains came down onto a gentle plain, I could see a few scattered roofs. Ruth ran ahead to catch up with Papa, leaving me with the cow, who now would not move at all unless I twisted her tail and hit her hard with a stick. The cow did not even seem thankful when I closed her in the large fenced meadow above the houses, where there was plenty of grass to eat. She stood looking after me as if to say, *This is it?*

This is it. I found our house, and Adar stood stiffly just inside the doorway. "How will we keep the wild animals out, with no windows or doors?"

"Are there wild animals?" Ruth asked anxiously.

With her jaw snapped tight, Adar handed Leb to Ruth and began sweeping our rough pine floor. She stopped a minute with her hands on her hips and looked around our small house. It had only one room with a cot along one wall, a cookstove in the corner, and a small wooden table and chairs.

"I will need water for scrubbing," Adar growled at me.

There is already a wild animal inside our house, I thought.

I grabbed two pails and hurried to the creek along the path Papa showed me. I found the place where a circle of stones had been placed to make a small pool and filled the first bucket, setting it carefully behind me on the bank.

As I turned to reach for the second pail, an icy chill prickled my spine. Only a few feet behind me, in the bushes near the creek, a brown furry face appeared. It sniffed the air, making low, grunting sounds.

Suddenly it stopped and stared at me with its round glassy

eyes. It reared up, snapping branches as it stood, then growled and swiped the air with its sharp-clawed front paws.

Quickly I looked around for something to throw. I grabbed the full pail of water and tossed it, bucket and all, at the bear, then ran toward the house without looking back.

"Where is my water?" Adar demanded.

Clutching my side, I gasped, "Bear!"

Ruth ran to the door to look, and Adar yanked her back by the collar, quickly glancing for something to block the door. We turned the table on its side, pushing it across the entrance, then huddled on Papa's cot, waiting for him to return.

"What has happened?" Papa asked when he came in a few minutes later. He leaned over the table, dropping the last of our bundles on the cabin floor.

I told him the story, and he said, "We will go back together for the water."

Even with Papa, I did not want to go back to the creek. I trailed behind him, trying not to think about the bear's teeth and sharp claws. When we got to the creek, we found the first, spilled bucket in the bushes and the second one near the water. Pressed into the mud along the bank was a paw print bigger than Papa's hand.

Papa was silent for a moment, then said, "The bear will not come back with so many people living here."

I did not know if I should listen to Papa's words or go by his actions. When we returned to the house, he loaded his pistol and placed it on the rafters above our doorway.

I cannot sleep. The barrel of Papa's pistol is staring at me like a big round eye, reflecting in the glow of our lamp. Papa sits at our table writing a letter to Grandma Rose, and his pen makes a loud scratching sound.

I wonder if he is telling Grandma Rose about the bear, or about our house that is so small you can jump across it. I wonder if he is telling her that her grandchildren must sleep on the floor because we have no beds, and that there is no way to keep out the wild animals because we have no windows or doors.

If I were writing the letter, I would cry big teardrops onto the page, and they would tell the whole story.

6

I am feeling sorry for Adar. She is trying hard to make our house kosher, but it is like the house has a mind of its own and will not cooperate. For an hour now, she has been rearranging our belongings. First one place, then another, then back again where they started. I am dizzy from watching.

"There are not enough places to put things," Adar said. "And if I put dishes aside for the holidays, we will not have enough to eat on for every day."

Adar tried again to rearrange the dishes on the shelves Papa had built. "And how will I wash them separately with only one washing and rinsing pan?"

"You can wash the washing pan," Ruth volunteered.

Adar frowned. "And here are the towels," she said, unpacking a small bundle. Mama had embroidered some of the edges blue and the others red so that we could tell which ones to use for *milchik*, the dairy foods, and which for *flayshig*, the meat. "If I put the towels for dairy over here and the towels for meat over here, I will have no place for the pots and pans."

"We have not been keeping kosher during our travels," I said.

33

"This is different." Adar refolded one of the dish towels. "This is our house!"

"When will Papa be back?" Ruth asked.

"In a little while," I said, thinking that when we were in Cotopaxi, we waited for Papa to come home from the mountains, and now we are waiting for him to come back from Cotopaxi. "He is bringing hinges so he can hang our door."

"So the bear won't come in our house and eat us?" Ruth said.

"The bear is gone," I told Ruth, sounding braver than I felt.

"Then what is that animal coming up the trail?"

I looked out and squinted. At first I did not know what it was, then saw it was Papa and Benjamin carrying an old and rusted bedstead. Ruth ran out to meet them, then came back shouting, "Papa and Benjamin have found a bed. It's for us!"

"You cannot just find a bed," Adar said.

"They did," Ruth said. "It was half buried in the sand. Someone just left it there."

Papa put together the frame and stood it in the corner where our blankets had been. He placed some rough boards across the frame, pushing them together to make a flat surface.

"But it has no mattress." Ruth pouted.

"It is better than the floor," Adar pointed out.

Ruth shifted from one foot to the other, looking at the bed. Just then a voice called into our house. As if in answer to our prayers, Rachel Schloff appeared in our doorway, holding the two extra blankets Papa had loaned her. "We won't be needing these now that the weather is warmer," she said.

34

"Papa, can we use them for a mattress?" I asked.

Papa agreed, and Adar set about sewing the blankets together to make a large square sack. "We will need some grass to fill it," she said.

Ruth and I took two old dresses and tied up the sleeves and necks to make bags for collecting. We passed Papa, who was already hammering the hinges our new door. "Make sure you do not pick the grass in the meadow where the milk cow grazes," he said.

We walked down the mountain, avoiding the thick trees where a bear might be hiding. We scavenged between bushes and in grassy spots where water collects when it snows. In one of these places, I reached down to pull some grass. There, in the shade of a wild rosebush, lay the spotted body of a newborn deer.

I waved Ruth over, and we crouched down to watch the sleeping fawn, curled up with its nose resting between its front hooves. "Do you think I can pet it?" she whispered.

I told her no, afraid it would wake, but I wanted to touch it, too. It made me think of things that are soft—the quilt for our bed, the silk cover for matzo, Mama's skin …

"Where do you think the mama deer is?" Ruth asked.

At that moment, the mother deer appeared through the nearby brush and stood just a few yards away. The noise of the rattling bushes surprised me, and I did not know what the deer would do. I grabbed Ruth's hand and pulled her away, backing up step by step.

When we were a safe distance from them, the deer nudged her baby, and the fawn stood on wobbly legs and followed its mama through the thick brush. The last thing we saw was its fuzzy tail wagging.

"Was the deer going to hurt us?" Ruth asked.

"I don't think so. She was protecting her baby."

"Like Mama protecting us when the soldiers came?"

I had not thought Ruth was old enough to remember. Many months before Leb was born, there was a pounding on our door. Papa and Adar were away, and so it was just the three of us, Mama mending and me trying to help Ruth learn to sew on a button.

Slowly Mama answered the door, and two armed soldiers stood there: a short man with a mustache and a taller man whose eyes looked like two black stones.

"We have come for the tax money," the short man said.

Mama looked quickly at Ruth and me, then back to the man. "We have already paid," she said.

"It is a new tax, and we must collect today." The man's words were as sharp as knives.

Ruth scurried over and grabbed Mama's skirt, hiding in the folds. "My husband is not home," Mama said firmly.

"We will see, then, what we can collect for ourselves." The soldiers pushed into the room, and the short one grabbed Ruth. The tall man with the stone eyes looked in my direction.

It happened so fast, even now I cannot believe it. Mama snatched Ruth back from the man and ran over to me, grabbing my hand and pulling me out of the house with her, screaming, as loudly as she could, "Help! Please help!"

The soldiers rushed out into the road behind Mama, but

already Mrs. Washer had come running, and Mr. Golman came from the other direction. In a moment, a small crowd had gathered, surrounding the soldiers and keeping them from leaving.

"What is it? What has happened?"

"My children," Mama said, squeezing my hand so hard it hurt, "the soldiers are going to harm them."

The man with the mustache straightened up. "We are collecting tax money."

"What tax is this?" Mr. Golman asked. "We have all paid."

The tall man looked sideways at the shorter one, then spoke. "It is a new tax. A tax for…"

"Robber!" Mr. Golman shouted.

"Liar!" Mrs. Washer raised her broom.

Someone threw a rock at them, and several others began shouting and hollering until the soldiers hurried away without even looking back.

Mama loosened her grip on my hand, and Ruth began to cry. "They are gone, now," Mama said. "I would never let them harm you."

"We were not going to hurt the fawn," Ruth said, reminding me that I was not in Kishinev but on a mountainside in America, looking for grass for our new bed. Ruth wiggled her hand free, and I realized I had been squeezing it tightly the way Mama had squeezed mine.

I stared at the place the fawn had been, then up at the mountain peaks. The sun hung just above the ridge. "Hurry! We're going to be late."

37

We grabbed a few more handfuls of grass as we ran up the hill, and entered the house just as Adar lit the Sabbath candle. Papa balanced Leb on one knee and frowned at us as we dropped our grass-filled dresses on the bed frame.

If only we had not stopped to look at the fawn, I thought. *If only I had paid more attention to the time.*

Papa began to recite the kiddush prayer, and when he got to the blessing of the wine, I blurted, "Papa, we have no wine!"

Papa looked sternly at me over the rims of his glasses. He lifted his cup of water and drank. Adar did the same, followed by Ruth, who did not mind pretending. He finished thanking the Lord for creating the Sabbath, then he said quietly to me, "For many things here, we will have to make do. Our house is small, and the little money we have must be spent to buy seed and get our farm started. God will understand if we bend a few rules."

Adar breathed a sigh of relief and looked over at the shelves where our dishes were stacked. She would no longer need to worry about separating our few plates for daily and special occasions, or keeping the towels separate, or two sets of silverware.

No matter what Adar does, Papa lets it pass. Leb, too, can do no wrong. And if Ruth makes a mistake, he pats her head and says, "Don't worry about it. You are still young."

With me it is different. No matter how hard I try, I cannot please Papa.

7

In the beginning, God created rocks. Round and smooth, rough and broken, sparkly and dull, pink, white, gray, and sand-colored and black. I have never seen so many rocks. Ever. They burrow out of the soil like little animals, and when I think I have found them all, a new one appears on the surface where I have already picked and picked one hundred times or more.

"Bring me the wheelbarrow," Etta called.

I rolled it over and we filled it with stones. Together we pushed it to the edge of the patch we were clearing for a garden. We stacked the larger rocks to make a wall and gave the smaller ones to Ruth and her friend Hazel, who carried them down the slope and dumped them in a pile.

Etta stopped a moment to wipe the sweat from her face with the edge of her sleeve. "If we don't get that plow soon, it will be too late to plant. Summer is already here."

"We have so little equipment, and it all must be shared," Sarah sighed.

"We were promised there would be enough for everyone."

Etta picked up the handles of the wheelbarrow and rolled it back to the center of the garden.

"The promises have blown away like dust in the wind."

At that moment, a little whirl of dust began to spin at the top of the garden patch. It spiraled toward us across the dry ground, lifting our skirts. I did not know then that the dust devil would be a bad omen for me.

At noontime, when we stopped to eat, Papa asked me if I could watch little Leb so that Adar could hike to the lower houses with a message.

"Please, Papa, let me take it," I begged. "I am sure I can remember the way."

Papa looked from Adar to me and back again.

"I am busy with the mending," Adar said sharply. "And Emma will tickle and play with Leb. After that he will not nap."

Papa drew a long breath and studied me. "It is a long walk," he said.

"I know, Papa."

"You must go right there and come straight home."

"I will, Papa."

Papa sat down at the table to write the note. He folded it and handed it to me. "I will tell Etta you will be back later to help her."

My heart flew with my feet down the trail. Papa would not be sorry he let me deliver the note, and the next time there was an important job to do, he would not waste time deciding which daughter would do it!

If only my feet had not been flying so fast. There were two

trails at the first ravine. I chose the one that went left and sloped down quickly. After a few minutes it disappeared, with nothing but a few deer droppings to show that it had even been there.

Never mind, I thought. *I will climb to the other side of the ravine and find the right trail again.* But when I reached the top, it was as if the great teacher and magical rabbi, the Bal Shem Tov, had woven a spell over the land and changed it into a strange and foreign place.

I looked over my shoulder in the direction from which I had come. The large bald mountain, which was just above our house, had not moved. A little voice inside me said, *Turn back. You have not come far.*

I should have listened to that voice. Instead, I felt the waist of my dress for the note Papa had given me and thought how proud he would be of me when I returned.

I looked in the direction I was going. Below, to my right, stretched a wide valley of green fields mingled with pinnacles of rock that rose up from the valley floor. One notched rock that looked like the tip of a crochet hook poked up above the others. To my left were the jagged peaks of the Blood of Christ Mountains. The other houses were in between, on the flat above Oak Grove Creek, where we first walked up from Cotopaxi. The houses would not be hard to find.

I set out cross-country, keeping the bald mountain to my left and the notched rock to my right. It was not long before the crochet hook vanished and my feet began to hurt. I stopped for a moment to rest, trying not to think about my toes pinching and heels rubbing inside my shoes. The bald mountain was still there, but the green fields and rock pinnacles were no more.

Finally I saw smoke—gray puffs floating upward at the far end of the little clearing where I walked. The houses! I ran, forgetting my sore toes and heels, forgetting my tiredness.

From a distance, I saw people standing near the flames of a small fire. If they were not from the houses, then they would be able to help me find them. I ran until the faint smell of smoke grew strong and kept on until I reached the fire.

There I stopped and clapped a hand over my mouth. A little scream started inside my throat and rose into my mouth, crouching there like a wildcat, ready to spring.

Two bloody men stood near the trees looking at me. They were naked from the waist up and held sharp knives with bone handles. A deer hung between them, strung by a rope, dangling from its hind legs.

For as long as I live, I will not forget the twisted red flesh of the animal's legs, nor the gray, limp deerskin that drooped down over its lolling head.

One of the men spoke. He pointed at me with his bloody knife and said words in a language that sounded like a dog growling.

A woman near the fire stood up and answered him. She wore a dress of soft leather, stretched tightly around her middle. Her hair hung in long black braids, and on one cheek there was a scar that started below her right eye and ended near her chin.

Nearby, a boy squatted by the fire, roasting a piece of red meat on a stick. He pulled it from the fire and began to eat, tearing the meat with his teeth, chewing slowly. He did not take his eyes off me.

I started to back away, but the man spoke again, motioning toward me with the blade of his knife. The woman and the boy moved away from the fire, and the man stepped forward. He spoke again, this time slowly in English.

Now, even if I had wanted to, I could not move. My feet were anchored by roots of fear. I don't know where my voice came from, but I yelled loudly in Yiddish, "I'm lost! I am with the Jewish people. I'm trying to find their houses."

The man lowered his knife, and the lines around his mouth softened. His black eyes flickered with amusement. He spoke again in his strange tongue to the people around him. One by one, like single drops of water, they began to chuckle. The woman with the scar on her face hid a smile behind her hand. Her chest heaved, and her dark eyes danced.

"Houses!" I tried to show them with my hands, drawing a square shape with a point at the top.

The laughter now sounded like a rolling creek, and the boy by the fire mimicked my speech, tucking his hands into his armpits and flapping his arms like a chicken.

I backed away slowly, step by step, then turned and fled, not caring where I went. I ran until my chest ached and my sides hurt.

Finally I stumbled and stopped to catch my breath, looking for the bald mountain and the rock that looked like a crochet hook.

Instead I saw Papa marching toward me along the trail. "Where have you been?" He frowned as he spoke.

43

Breathlessly I tried to explain about losing my way and about the smoke.

"The houses are just over there." Papa pointed.

I stared in disbelief at the rooftops and black stovepipes with wisps of smoke curling from them.

"But, Papa ..." I fingered the folds of the note, realizing that he had just come from the houses and delivered the message himself.

On the way back up the hill, Papa did not speak. I limped behind him with my heels burning and my toes grating on the fronts of my shoes.

"Papa, can we rest?" I asked, when the pain was too great. We were at the place where I had lost the trail, and I pointed to the second path, hoping he would understand how I had gotten lost.

Papa studied the two trails, walking down the second one and hiking back again. He took a handkerchief from his pocket and tied it to a low bush next to the trail we were on.

I looked at the handkerchief a moment and saw Papa's name where Mama had embroidered it. "Papa, it is the one Mama made for you."

He looked at me sadly. "It is better you do not get lost again. Come. Already much of the day has been wasted."

I struggled up and followed Papa. Now when I walked, my feet throbbed with pain. Tears filled my eyes, but I wiped them away, not wanting him to see me cry. I hobbled after him, counting every step to our door.

"Papa should have asked me to go," Adar said when she saw

me. "Or Ruth. Even she would have been able to find the way!"

I was too tired to remind Adar that she had not wanted to go, that she had wanted to stay home and sew and watch little Leb.

Adar warmed a pan of salt water and poured it slowly over my feet. I bit my lip, trying hard not to cry. My toes and heels were bloody where the blisters had broken. The salt stung.

"Why didn't you tell Papa your shoes were too small?" As if Adar needed something else to scold me about.

Just then Papa came in carrying a pair of hand-me-down shoes from Etta. "These will have to do," he said.

I looked at the battered and scuffed shoes and could no longer hold back my misery. I sobbed loudly, the tears spilling down my cheeks making enough salty water to fill another pan.

At that moment little Leb pulled himself onto my lap. I cuddled and rocked him, crying even harder. When I finally stopped, Leb touched a chubby hand to my wet cheek. "Ma-ma-ma." It was his way of saying Emma. I know he was trying to make me feel better, but he only made me cry harder, wishing I was small again, sitting on my own mama's lap.

Adar complains because she has to go outside and help plant the potatoes instead of staying in the house with little Leb.

"It must be nice," she says, "to sit around soaking your feet while I sweat in the garden."

"I would rather plant potatoes," I tell her, thinking that when she is watching Leb, she calls it hard work, but when it is my turn, she says it is easy.

It is not easy at all. Leb wobbles and bounces from one place to another like the marionette puppet we saw on the street corner in New York City. He is up and down and up again, always moving. And it does no good to close the door. He climbs up to the open windows, and I have to pull him down again.

"Windows of air," Ruth calls them.

"Windows we can afford," Papa says.

It is better to take Leb outside to play. He digs with an old spoon in the dirt and picks up small rocks and brings them to me, scurrying back and forth until we have made a small pile.

He reminds me of the little chipmunk that comes to the place near our door where we throw our dishwater. The chipmunk looks for small bits of food, and when he finds a scrap, he sits up on his hind legs, holding the morsel between his paws, chittering.

On days when we are not outside, he comes to our front door, and Ruth feels sorry for him and drops small crumbs of bread for him to eat. Papa does not know about it, or he would scold her for wasting food.

I am hoping tomorrow Papa will let me work in the garden again. I think he will, as long as I keep my feet covered and do not get dirt in my last blister. That means I will have to wear Etta's shoes, which look like two rotting potatoes.

"It's better than shoes that pinch your toes and rub your heels raw," Adar said when I complained.

I know this is true, but I don't want to give up my old ones. They remind me of shopping with Mama just before Leb was born.

"I want them a little big," Mama told the cobbler as he measured my feet. "She is growing."

"And you," Mr. Nilva said with a wink. He was talking about Mama's stomach, which was round as a bread bowl.

Mr. Nilva stood up and looked at his shelves, fingering the end of his gray beard thoughtfully. "I think I have a pair, ready-made, that will fit." He took them from the top shelf.

Mama frowned. She had been selling bread and saving her shekels in a jar for weeks until she had enough. "We have three girls to clothe. The shoes are much too fancy."

"They have been here growing dust," Mr. Nilva said. "I can give you a good price."

Mama folded her arms and rested them on her stomach. After a long moment she said, "Let's see if they will fit."

Mr. Nilva handed me the shoes, and I tried them on, pulling the laces tight. Even so, my feet slipped around loosely inside. "They are only a little big," I lied, knowing that if I did not get these I would have to wear plain leather boots that pulled on and did not tie. "I will grow fast!" I added. "And I can pass the shoes to Ruth when I have outgrown them."

Mama smiled at me and dug into her purse, counting the money she had saved. She did not have enough.

"You can pay me the rest with your fresh bread," Mr. Nilva said.

Mama agreed, and I hurried home to show off my new shoes to Adar and Ruth.

"Since when are you so special?" Adar said. "Can I have them when they are too small for you?" Ruth asked.

I told her yes, then looked over to see Mama clutch her stomach. The color drained from her face.

Later that night little Leb was born. His first loud screams woke us.

"Is the baby okay?" Ruth asked.

"Go back to sleep," Adar said. "You screamed, too, when you were born."

Baby Leb was healthy, but Mama was so weak she could not talk. She only squeezed my hand a little when I visited her.

A week later, I asked Mr. Nilva if he would like me to bake him some bread. He said, "I can wait until your mama is better."

We waited for weeks for Mama to get better, but she did not. When she tried to get out of bed, her face turned gray and her legs folded under her. Every day we brought little Leb to her so she could feed him. One day she could not even hold him in her arms.

After she died, I baked bread for Mr. Nilva, but he would not take it. "All your mama's debts on this earth have been paid," he said.

It is a good thing he did not take the bread. Ruth almost cried when she ate it. "It doesn't taste like Mama's," she whined.

It is true. Nothing has been the same since Mama died. I would not want her to see the shoes now. There is nothing left of them to pass down to Ruth.

8

Just when Papa had forgotten about my getting lost, I have upset him again. I wish I had stayed home with Adar and Ruth, but when Papa asked me if I would go with him to Cotopaxi to help Etta clean our new synagogue, I could not say no.

If only Etta had not been so picky about the walls! If she had just said, "They are fine. Now we can rest." Instead she stood with her hands on her hips, looking for specks of dirt we had missed. Her brow wrinkled and her lip curled into a frown. "We need to wash them one more time."

I looked over at Papa and Benjamin, hoping they would spare me, but Benjamin was hammering together the last of the benches and Papa was measuring the boards for the table at the front of the synagogue that would hold our sacred scrolls.

"I need the water today, not tomorrow." Etta handed me the bucket to fill.

I hurried out the door, passed Mr. Black's store, and continued to the creek beyond the hotel where we first stayed. It was on the way back that I noticed the horse with the white star on its head, tied to the hitching rail outside the hotel. His tail swished lazily in the sunshine, and I could not resist stopping for a moment to stroke his soft coat.

I plunked down the bucket and the water splattered up with a loud splash. The sound startled the horse, and it jumped backward from the rail, jerking the reins free.

"*Gevalt!*" I yelled, thinking someone would come from the hotel to help, but I only frightened the horse more, and it trotted away toward the creek.

"Horse! Horse!" I shouted again, using the English word I had learned from the boy. The horse stopped, so I tiptoed slowly over, thinking I would catch it. Almost … almost… I had the reins in my fingers, then the horse shied away, hopping sideways like Ruth when she plays tag with Hazel.

Water sprayed me as the horse tromped across the creek and galloped up the hill beyond the hotel. I ran after it until we reached the small cemetery where the hill crested. There the horse stopped to nibble the sprigs of green grass growing between a few scattered grave markers.

Now is my chance, I thought.

Barely breathing, I crept up beside the horse and grabbed the reins, holding tightly as he pulled away from me.

"Now I must take you back," I said, feeling proud of myself for catching him. Then I looked back down the hill toward the hotel, thinking Etta must be getting tired of waiting for me. If I rode the horse back, it would be much faster, and maybe she would not even know I had been gone.

I did not think it would be hard to do. I put the reins around the horse's neck, stood on tiptoe, and stretched up for the stirrup.

At that moment, the horse stepped away from me. I fell backward, bumping hard on the ground next to a little white cross. The horse galloped away down the hill toward the hotel, kicking up small stones as it went.

I stood and limped after it, afraid now that the horse would be lost forever. It would be my fault, and I did not know how I would explain it to Papa.

My heart fell when I came around the front of the hotel. Papa and Etta were both there, staring at the bucket of water near the hitching rail. Right next to them was the horse, shifting its weight from foot to foot as if it had been standing there all day.

"I have been looking everywhere for you!" Etta cried.

I pointed to the horse and up the hill, trying to explain what had happened.

Etta looked at the horse standing calmly and shook her head. "It does not look like a runaway horse to me. *Luftmensh.* Silly girl. I think you have your head in the clouds."

I stared at the ground, waiting for Papa to speak.

At that moment the front door of the hotel swung open and Mr. Black stepped out. He walked over to the horse, picked up the reins, and slid up into the saddle, nodding to us as he turned the horse and rode off.

"The horse ran away?" Papa asked with a confused look on his face.

"Yes, Papa."

"All the way up the hill to the cemetery?"

"Yes, Papa."

He looked at the place where the horse had been standing and then back at me. He did not look through his glasses, but over the rims, with a long, slow stare.

I swallowed hard, knowing he did not believe what I was telling him.

"And then the horse came back here?"

"Yes, Papa." The toes of Etta's shoes began to blur as I studied them. I wished I had hurried back with the water. I wished I had not seen the horse.

Papa sighed, and it was loud like a rushing wind. He turned away from me and walked back to the synagogue, shaking his head.

When we got back home, Ruth began asking questions about the new synagogue.

"When will I get to see it?"

"On Friday," I told her, "when we dedicate our sacred scroll."

"What does it look like?"

I did not want to disappoint her by saying it was just a little shack behind Mr. Black's store—that it was not like any synagogue she had ever seen. "It is very clean," I said.

Next Ruth asked about the large canopy Adar was sewing. "When will it be finished?"

Adar looked up from the yards of white fabric that lay on her lap. She was carefully stitching a scallop around the edge of the chuppah that would be part of the procession. "I am working as fast as I can."

"What about the poles to hold the chuppah up?"

"Papa and the men will cut them from trees."

"And when it is finished, will it be used for weddings, too?"

Adar put down her needle and sighed. "It will be used for all the important ceremonies."

Ruth did not ask any more questions until we arrived at the synagogue on Friday and formed a line outside the door. Papa stood in front with the other men and elders. We stood behind with Adar and little Leb and the other women and children, waiting for the sun to go down.

"When are we going to start moving?" Ruth asked.

"Shhhh!" I held a finger to my lips. I knew Papa would be angry with me if I did not keep Ruth still during the ceremony for our Sefer Torah. The sacred scroll had come all the way from New York, and without it our synagogue would not be complete.

"I can't see." This time Ruth stood on tiptoe and whispered in my ear.

"There's not much to see," I whispered back. Heads and heads and more heads. I could just barely see the back of Papa's prayer shawl and the scalloped edge of the chuppah, which wiggled on one corner.

"Why are the Calof boys holding the chuppah?" Ruth asked.

"Because they are single men."

Ruth giggled at this, and said, "Noah is only a little older than me."

"Mochel cannot hold up the canopy by himself," I said. "It takes four." The wiggly corner of the chuppah dipped downward.

53

"Why are all those people watching us?"

I looked over and noticed for the first time that a group of local people had gathered near Mr. Black's store. I did not know the answer to this.

"Why doesn't everyone have candles?" Ruth wondered.

"Just the elders. It is part of the ceremony."

"When are we going to start?" Ruth asked me again.

"Shhhh!" I looked at the sun balancing on the ridge to the west. Like a stubborn child, it refused to go down.

Just then, a stillness passed over us. I could smell the scent of burning candles and hear Papa's voice lift in a melodious chant. We began to move forward, and Ruth's eyes grew wide. She squeezed my hand. It seemed we floated into the synagogue on God's palm.

Papa and the other men recited the Psalms and prayers, and finally the Ark that contained the Torah was opened, and the scroll set in its place. For a long moment I became lost in the candlelight, and I could not tell where I stopped and the other people began. The chanting filled the room, and we were the flames, flickering together as one glowing light.

When we stepped outside after the service, I expected Ruth to start jabbering again. Instead, she walked in a silent trance beside me. She did not say anything until we got to the hotel's dining room, where a meal had been prepared for us, roast chicken and carrot tzimmes that melted in my mouth.

"The carrots taste like Mama's," Ruth said.

"Almost."

I was still thinking about Mama when I walked out into

the warm summer evening and looked over at the area where the dancing had begun. For a moment I could not move. There stood Mama in the light of the rising moon, wearing her favorite white blouse with the high lacy collar. Her hair was pulled back and bundled into a knot.

I could not think why Mama did not have her head covered. Always, when she was out, she wore her wig or a scarf. Then I realized it was not Mama but Adar at the edge of the dancers, stealing glances at Mochel Kahn, trying to catch his eye.

It should be Mama, I thought. *She should be here with us. She should be standing in the moonlight, just like Adar, waiting to dance with Papa.*

People began to laugh. I hurried closer in time to see Leb twirling and twirling like a plump little dreidel.

A moment later he fell with a thump. His eyes grew round as the moon, and I thought he would cry. Instead, he picked himself up, clapped his pudgy hands, and began twirling again. Papa scooped him up and tossed him toward the sky. He fell into Papa's arms, giggling, and Papa tossed him up again.

"I do not feel well," Ruth said, holding her stomach.

"What have you been eating?" I asked suspiciously, looking at the rim of frosting around her mouth.

"Nothing," Ruth said, but crumbs fell from the pocket where she had hidden an extra sweet cake.

It was late when we started for home. The peaks were silhouetted in the moonlight, and the trail glowed like a silvery carpet. Papa swung Leb over one shoulder and carried him up the hill, sound asleep. Papa chanted as we hiked, and his voice echoed from the Blood of Christ Mountains into the valley below.

The coyotes answered him with their own song, howling into the night.

Soon we passed the handkerchief Papa had tied on the bush near the place where I had lost the trail. After only a few weeks, it was thin and fraying, but I could still see Mama's small, neat stitches where she had embroidered Papa's name.

Suddenly I felt all alone. The white handkerchief moved a little in the moonlight like a ghost, reminding me of Mama.

My heart ached. I wanted to take the frayed cloth and hold it close to me. I did not want to leave it hanging there alone on the bush. I looked backward as we passed by. Papa's chanting faded away, and all I could hear was the long, eerie song of the coyotes.

9

Adar has been acting strangely. Every time Mochel comes to our house to speak with Papa, she smoothes her apron and tucks in stray strands of hair. Then she busies herself straightening blankets on the bed and organizing the shelves that store our food—things she never does—and pretends she has no ears.

She does. Her ears work like colanders, catching and rinsing information, listening for the mention of her name.

Today Mochel came to our house when Papa was not home. Adar told him a mild little lie, saying he would be back soon, and she offered Mochel a cup of coffee.

Ruth's eyes grew round as saucers, and she opened her mouth to speak, but Adar shushed her with a look that would make a stone quiver. Even Ruth knew that Papa had left early to get supplies and would not be back until late.

Mochel sat stiff-backed at our table, waiting. This time, Adar did not busy herself with cleaning but sat down across from him, bossing Ruth and me until she ran out of things for us to do. In between her bossing, she chattered like the chipmunk that comes to our door, looking for food. She only stopped once, and that was when little Leb pulled himself up to an empty window and poked his head over the edge.

"Watch the baby," she said to me and then continued to talk, not noticing Mochel's empty cup or the tap, tap, tapping of his foot against the leg of the table.

Finally Mochel cleared his throat and stood up, pulling nervously on the sleeve of his shirt.

Adar stopped talking, flushing pink. "I'm sorry Papa is not back," she said, standing to walk him to the door. "I'll tell him you were here."

Mochel said, "Thank you," and nodded. It was the first two words he had been able to squeeze in.

Nothing around here is a secret. Later, when I went to work in the garden, I heard about the visit from Etta Stokes. "I saw Mochel leaving your house today," she said, kneeling down to start weeding a row of carrots. "Your papa wasn't there."

I did not know how to answer, so I moved down my row a little, pretending to look for weeds under the spinach greens that were just beginning to leaf out.

"I think she is going to have a broken heart," Etta continued. "Mochel has eyes for only one girl … and a married one at that."

"Feh!" Sarah Luper moved to my row and knelt down, working behind me to pull the weeds I'd missed. "You mean the marriage between Mindel and Jonas Solomon? It wasn't a proper marriage—not one recognized by God."

Etta snorted. "If it was recognized by Mindel, I doubt whether God or Mochel can undo it," she said.

58

"Mochel's going to try," said Sarah. "He came all the way to America to win her back."

"There is no telling what young people today will do." Etta gave me a stern look before inching down the row.

"Just as I was saying." Sarah bumped me and moved around to stay within talking distance of Etta. "Mindel defied the matchmaker twice and then came to America to be married by a justice of the peace. No synagogue or rabbi."

It was me now, scooting down the row to make sure I did not miss a word. This was the same Mindel and Jonas that Sarah and Etta were talking about the day we walked up from Cotopaxi. That night, I had asked Papa about them. "Ignore the gossip," he'd said. "Unkind words are like weeds in a garden. If you are not careful, they will spread and take over."

I looked at Etta and Sarah, thinking the weeds of gossip were spreading rapidly. It has been this way since the arrival of Mindel and Jonas two days ago—like stinging hornets have arrived to stir things up.

"A broken heart," Etta repeated. "Your sister should not get her hopes up."

When I returned to the house, I told Adar what Etta and Sarah had said. "They think you should forget about Mochel Kahn."

Adar turned on me. "What do you know of it?" she demanded. "Your head is as empty as our windows of air."

"It's true," I protested. "Mindel was promised to Mochel long before we left home, and he has come all the way here to America to get her back." That is when Adar bumped the table, and our best mixing bowl fell and shattered on the floor.

"It's not fair that one girl should have so many suitors!" Ignoring the broken bowl, Adar picked up the wooden spoon and waved it at me.

I stooped to pick up the large fragments of pottery, wishing I had heeded Papa's words about spreading gossip. Thorny weeds filled our house.

"Perhaps it is not true," I said, sorry I had upset Adar. "Perhaps it is just two old kibitzers who should mind their own business."

"No," Adar said, her voice breaking. "It is true. I know it is. There is no hope for me."

Ruth brought over the broom and helped me sweep. When I looked up, Adar was wiping her eyes with the sleeve of her blouse. I have never seen Adar cry, not ever—not even when Mama died.

"It is just gossip," I said, feeling worse than ever. I handed Adar the dish towel so she would not have to use her sleeve.

She pushed my hand away and said, "Don't worry about me. I will not crack and fall to pieces like the bowl."

I carried the broken shards out to the dumping spot behind our houses. It started as a big empty hole. Now it is filling with bits and pieces of broken dreams.

Two days later I found out that Etta was right about Adar's heart. If it is not broken, then at least it has a very large bruise. Adar has not spoken a kind word to anyone, snapping like the little traps Papa sets to keep the mice away from our grain.

Since the arrival of Mindel and Jonas, all the talk has been about whether or not they have been properly married.

"They have only a paper signed by a justice of the peace," Etta said. "That cannot be a marriage recognized by God."

Mochel has been to our house, asking Papa how to get the marriage annulled, and Adar has had to listen to this, sitting like a stone on our bed, as there is nowhere else to go.

I don't understand why everyone is so upset about Jonas and Mindel. They are grown up, but people treat them like little children who have behaved badly. I do not dare say this, especially in front of Adar. She is like a violin string that has been stretched too tight. One more turn and she will fly to pieces.

Papa does not take sides, even though I know he must be losing his patience with all the people who have come here to consult with him. Our house has more people than the train station in New York City. There does not seem to be any agreement.

"Mindel does not have her head covered," Etta said, planting more seeds in the garden of gossip. "Not even a scarf!"

"You see? She is not truly married," Sarah replied.

"They have a signed paper," Rachel pointed out.

"An American justice of the peace is not the same as a rabbi."

"Where can you find a rabbi in all these rocks?" Etta plucked a small stone from under her and tossed it to the edge of the garden.

I looked up from my weeding and saw Mindel standing near the place where the rock had landed, talking to Mochel Kahn. I could not hear what they were saying, but Mochel's hands were clasped tightly as if in prayer, and he had a look of pleading on his face. Mindel shook her head, and he slowly turned and walked away.

Etta had been watching, too. "Hmmmf." She started to speak, but Mindel came toward us. She knelt down next to Etta and began pulling weeds. All the talking stopped; it was so quiet you could hear the weeds weep.

Mindel broke the silence. "I am sorry we could not have come earlier to help with the planting. Jonas needed to finish his job in Leadville."

I did not know weeds could be so interesting. Etta studied each one as she pulled. Rachel finished a row and walked away.

After another long silence, Mindel added, "It is so good to be here. I have missed my family."

"You did not think of your family when you came to America without your father's permission," Sarah blurted. "And Jonas, too, should be ashamed."

"I have spoken with Father," Mindel said. "Jonas and I are planning a wedding in the new synagogue."

"And then will you cover your hair in the proper manner?" Etta stood and dusted off her skirt.

I could not believe what Mindel answered. "We are in America now. We can change old traditions."

The weed Sarah held slipped from her fingers, and her

mouth fell open. She touched her head to make sure her head scarf was still in place.

"I knew a Jewish factory worker in New York," Mindel continued, "who was nearly crushed when her head scarf was caught in a machine. It is dangerous to work with one on."

"It is not a factory here," Etta snapped. "And we are not in New York City." She put both hands on her hips and glanced around. "We are … we are …"

Beyond the garden wall, we could see the green valley floor and rocky hills. Behind us, the Blood of Christ Mountains made a jagged wall that could not be crossed. For once, Etta was speechless.

"Minnie … ," Jonas called, and waved from the edge of the garden.

Etta and Sarah stared blankly at each other as Mindel went over and spoke to him. "Who is Minnie?" they grumbled when she returned.

"Minnie is my American name. It is easier for people here to remember."

"And harder for us," Sarah said.

"My name is Emma," I said, trying to say something polite.

Minnie smiled at me, and I knew already that I would like her.

Just then, Ruth arrived with a bucket of cold drinking water. Mindel took the dipper and filled it, offering it first to Etta and then to Sarah.

Next, Mindel offered the ladle to me. "Thank you, Minnie," I said.

"Minnie. Hmmmph." Sarah frowned.

"Young people," Etta said. Her eyes fixed on me. "They have no respect."

Sarah and Etta picked up their hoes and began swinging them furiously, making the dirt fly as they moved down the row away from us.

"Is something the matter?" Ruth asked.

Minnie smiled and roughed Ruth's hair. "Thank you for the water," she said, first in Yiddish and then in English.

"Thank you for the water," I said, copying Minnie.

Ruth looked confused for a moment, then said, "You're welcome," in Yiddish. Minnie told her how to say it in English, and she tried it. "You are welcome."

It sounded stiff and choppy, but Ruth gave me the courage to try. "You are wel ... come," I said.

Minnie smiled again. "I will teach you more English when there is time."

"Me, too?" Ruth asked.

"Anyone who would like to learn. We can meet over there." She pointed to the rock wall at the lower end of our garden. "But only when the work is finished."

"Thank you," I told her in English.

10

Things could not get any worse for Adar.
Mochel Kahn came to our house this morning to say good-bye.
He carried a large bundle, which he set down in our doorway
while he hugged Papa.

"Will you send word when you arrive in Denver?" Papa
asked him.

Mochel nodded. "I will find work there, and then I will send
for my brother to join me."

"If we had money to help pay for the train …" Papa's words
trailed off.

"I can walk," Mochel said with determination. "I will make it."

I stared past Mochel out our door at the mountain they
call Pikes Peak and thought of the Indians and bears and
rattlesnakes in the rugged country. I could not imagine anyone
walking all the way to Denver.

"God willing, you will be safe."

"God willing."

All this time, Adar did not come to the door but stood
at the stove with her back to us, stirring and stirring. When

Mochel left she said, "The bears can eat him for all I care."

A few minutes later, Rachel came to our house, taking up a collection for Mindel's dowry.

"The wedding will be held in two weeks," she said. "This time everything will be done properly."

"We have nothing," Adar said shortly.

"A small spoon or extra pan?" Rachel asked. "Or white cloth to make a wedding dress?"

Adar folded her arms across her chest. The look on her face told Rachel that she should leave.

"I know of something," Ruth said.

Before Adar could stop her, she skipped to our trunk and came back carrying a white linen tablecloth that was much too large for our small table.

Rachel looked back and forth from Adar to me, waiting for someone to speak.

My tongue froze, and a knot twisted in my stomach. I did not want to be the one to decide if Mama's tablecloth would go or stay.

For a long moment I stared at the weave of the cloth, remembering how it looked spread on our dining-room table at home, set with Mama's special dishes for the Sabbath meal. I could see the candlelight reflected off our glassware, and a room that danced with sparkles of light.

One night Grandma Rose and Grandpa Abraham were with us, and at the last minute, Uncle Zadok and his family arrived. It was the first night Mama and Papa spoke of moving to America.

"It is not right that Jews cannot own land," Uncle Zadok said. "The soldiers came and told us we had three days to pack up and leave."

"And your crops?" Mama asked. "Will they be left to wither?"

"No," Uncle Zadok said. "I have come to ask you to keep my family. I am going back to harvest my crops." Aunt Leah's face was as white as our tablecloth.

"It's too risky," Papa said. "You will lose everything… including your life."

Uncle Zadok frowned. "I have already lost everything."

"Not everything." Mama looked around the table at my five cousins. They stared quietly at their plates.

"People have been moving to America," Papa said. "They say there is land there for farming. They do not care, in America, if you are Jewish or Irish or Italian. If you work hard, you can own land. No one can take it away from you."

"I have worked hard here," Zadok said. "I do not want to give up what is justly mine."

"Please think about it," Aunt Leah pleaded.

"I have already spent too many sleepless nights thinking about it." Zadok turned to Papa and Mama. "Can my family stay here until I come back for them?"

"Your family is welcome," Mama said, placing our food on the table. "But …" The worry on her face finished her thought.

Uncle Zadok left the next morning. A week later, a small group of soldiers came to our door and told Papa that Uncle Zadok had been arrested. They took away Leah and the children and would not tell us where they were going. We never saw them again.

I looked down at the tablecloth in Ruth's hands. I wanted to say no like Adar had, then I thought of Mama placing the food on the table, making it stretch for Uncle Zadok and his family. Mama would never turn away someone in need. Never.

I took a long breath and said to Rachel, "You can have the tablecloth."

Adar frowned at me, and after Rachel left she said, "You would give away your own sisters if you could."

It was not easy to give away Mama's tablecloth, to see one more of her things disappear. But I could not say no. If someone else comes to our door and needs help, I will say yes.

Ruth pulled little Leb from the windowsill where he had climbed up, then bounced excitedly on the bed. "I can't wait to see the dress when it is finished."

"It will have a big red stain on it where you spilled beets," Adar said.

Ruth frowned. "It is only a small spot."

Adar gathered our breakfast dishes, which had not yet been washed, and dropped them into the wash pan as if we had plenty to spare. "By the time I am married there will be nothing left to wear but rags."

"Who are you going to marry?" Ruth asked in surprise.

Adar spun around with her hands dripping dish water. She walked over to Ruth and raised them like claws above her head. "If we stay up here on this mountain, it will be a large hairy bear, and I will have babies that look like wild animals!"

Ruth's eyes filled with tears.

"It is not Ruth's fault Jonas and Minnie are getting married," I said. "You are so grouchy, I am surprised there is not a line of bears outside our door asking Papa for your hand."

Adar slammed another dish into the pan and turned her back on us. "Mindel, Minnie," she grumbled. "Too many suitors. Too many names. I will just be Adar, stranded up here forever, waiting and waiting."

Adar's humor did not improve on the long walk to Cotopaxi on the day of the wedding. She trudged behind Papa, who carried Leb, and her face looked more ferocious than the growly bear she planned to marry. It did not help that the hot summer sun beat down on us.

I stayed back with Ruth, glad to have her for company. She skipped at my side, anxious for the food and dancing that would follow the ceremony. Her good mood spread to me, and when we arrived at the synagogue, I wanted to sing like the little yellow bird sitting in a cedar tree next to the sunny spot where the wedding would be held.

"See? The beet juice is hidden," Ruth whispered to me as Minnie made her seven circles around the wedding canopy. "Just as I told you."

Ruth was right. The dress did not look like someone's used tablecloth. Bits of lace and trim had been added to the collar and pleated front. Minnie wore a veil that had been made from pieced-together white linen scraps.

Papa read the seven wedding blessings, and when he came to the part about "sounds of joy and rejoicing," the little yellow bird made a whistling sound that trilled up and down the scale. A tear slid down Adar's cheek, and I could finally understand why she wanted so badly to be married.

"Mazel tov!" everyone shouted, and the little bird flew up and left us.

As it did, I heard Etta say, "It has finally been done properly."

"Amen," Sarah replied.

"I wish we had a wedding every day," Ruth said.

"Amen."

People began to clap, and there was a request for the parents of the bride and groom to begin the dancing. When they stopped, Papa smiled and made a toast to the newlyweds and laughed at the jokes made by the people around him.

Isaac Kessel, who is a widower like Papa, stood nearby with his two little girls. He made a second toast, and when he was finished, he walked over and stood next to Adar, continuing to talk. In a minute, she smiled, too.

If a wedding could make Adar smile, I thought, I would be like Ruth and wish for one every day.

Then I noticed Mr. Black walk over to the edge of the wedding party. He spoke to Benjamin Stokes, and together they waved Papa over. The smile on Papa's face faded. He followed Benjamin and Mr. Black from the party, leaving the laughing dancers behind.

"Where is Papa going?" Ruth asked.

"Stay here," I told her. I followed Papa, hanging near the bushes in case he looked back. I did not have far to go. Papa turned at Mr. Black's store and disappeared around to the front.

I should go back, I thought. It was the same little voice that spoke to me the day I got lost. I heard boots clomping on the wooden porch, then a rattling door.

I stood for a moment, at the side of the building, deciding what to do. I could hear voices through the open window just above my head. It was Papa and Benjamin and Mr. Black. Then a fourth voice joined in … a voice I had heard before.

I stretched up on tiptoe, using the windowsill to steady myself. Bolts of cloth were rolled and stacked high on the shelves of the opposite wall. There was another window below the shelves, but I was too short to see Papa.

A large round stone lay only a few feet away. I rolled it over below the window and stepped up on it. Now I could see clearly into the room, to the far side where four men sat at a small table. The fourth man was Mr. Reis … the man from the hotel … the man who left our houses unfinished.

Mr. Black cleared his throat and opened a tall flat book, and Papa took some papers from his pocket and unfolded them on the table. That is when a fear began to creep inside me, thinking about that morning when I found Papa at our table, sound asleep, with his head resting on our Bible.

One arm was draped over a pile of papers, and his hand curled around his pen. When I tried to wake him, I could see rows of numbers on the papers … the same papers he had now.

"In a few weeks," Papa said, "our crops will be harvested, and we will have enough money to pay our debt."

The rock wobbled beneath me, and I lost my balance, tipping sideways. I pulled myself up just as Benjamin had finished translating this for him.

Mr. Black shook his head gravely, staring at his black ledger. "It is almost August. The harvest will not be until September," he said. "I have already given you more credit than I should."

Papa tapped his foot against the table leg. After a long silence, the fourth man, Mr. Reis spoke. "I'm in need of workers in my mines. With jobs, you can extend your credit."

"For what pay?" Papa asked.

"One dollar and fifty cents a day. If your people will work at night, I can pay more."

Papa shook his head. "And who will harvest our crops if we are all working in your mine?"

The rock rolled again. This time it bumped the side of the building, making a loud clonking sound. I ducked my head and held my breath, hoping no one had noticed me.

"It is not our problem how you harvest your crops," Mr. Reis said stonily. "Your credit has run out."

Slowly, I inched up again and peeked over the sill. Papa fingered the breast pocket of his coat and pulled out a piece of velvet tied with string. When he unwrapped it, I could see the glow of Mama's wedding ring.

I let out a little gasp and tipped sideways again, grabbing the sill to keep from falling. I pulled myself up in time to hear Papa say, "I can offer this as a guarantee"—he paused—"until our harvest is in."

I clung to the sill, digging in with my fingernails, afraid to watch and afraid to look away.

Mr. Black took the ring from Papa and held it up in the light from the opposite window. Little sunbeams danced through it. He spoke in English to Mr. Reis, who did not look happy with what Mr. Black said.

Next, Mr. Black spoke to Papa. "If you cannot pay your bill, I will have to keep the ring."

Papa nodded.

"Mr. Reis can guarantee you a wage. Are you sure?"

"We have come here to farm," Papa said firmly.

Mr. Black rewrapped Mama's ring in the cloth and took it to his cash register. Papa turned away, and for a moment I thought he was looking at me, but he was staring at the grooves in Mr. Black's floor so that he would not have to watch Mama's ring disappear.

I said a silent prayer as the drawer of the cash register slid shut. *Please, God, make the beans and potatoes grow fast.*

I had not yet said, *Amen,* when a voice boomed at me. "There you are!" Etta's yell rolled the rock out from under me. I fell backward, bumping the windowsill with my head as I went down. "I have been looking everywhere for you."

I stood and dusted off my dress, quickly trying to think of a reason why I was there, but Etta was too busy scolding me to wait for an answer. "What kind of girl are you, who wanders off whenever she pleases? First it is a horse, and now you are going to tell me that the window of Mr. Black's store called you over."

I followed Etta back to the wedding party, holding my head with one hand. *We will have a good harvest,* I told myself. *I will work extra hard hoeing and pulling weeds. I will talk to the*

73

cabbages and sing to the beans. I will pray for sunshine, warm weather, and rain.

"What happened to your head?" Ruth asked when she saw me.

"It is nothing," I told her, but my head did not agree. It throbbed and pounded. I could not even enjoy the rest of the wedding party.

11

"Yes," "no," "please," and "thank you"; "How much does that cost?"; "I will give you one dollar."

These are the things we have been learning when we meet with Minnie for our English lessons. For two weeks now, since the wedding, we have been sitting near the garden wall in the evening, practicing words and phrases. At first Adar did not want to have anything to do with Minnie, but when she heard Ruth and me practicing, I think she could not stand to be left out.

"What are you saying?" Adar asked.

"Nothing," I said.

"It cannot be nothing. I am hearing words coming from your mouth."

"It is just everyday things," I told her. "How to greet people and how to shop and buy things."

"Hmmmf."

Ruth and I continued to practice.

"Now what are you saying?" Adar stopped sweeping and scowled at us.

"The same," I said. "But we are pretending to buy different things."

"It is not polite to talk like that in front of someone else."

"Talk like what?" I asked.

"Like what you are doing."

I did not know how to answer her, so it was a good thing Ruth spoke. "You should come learn English, too," she said. "Then you can practice with us."

"Hmmmf." Adar turned her back on us and swished her broom noisily.

The next evening Adar came with Leb to the garden wall and told us, "I just want to see what is going on."

That is when Ruth screamed.

At first I thought she saw a snake, but when I looked at what was coming up the trail, it was all I could do to keep from screaming, too. Adar turned as pale as barley soup, then she faltered, groping for the wall to keep from falling. I had to grab little Leb to keep him from hitting his head.

It was the blood that did it. I don't know which was worse—the blood on the horse or the blood on the face of the man limping toward us.

Minnie is the only one of us who managed to stay calm. She took the reins of the horse from the man and made him sit down, then she sent Ruth for Etta and Papa and told her to bring back a pail of clean water and something to make bandages with.

The man did not have his senses. He kept muttering the same English words over and over again. I asked Minnie what he meant, but she frowned and told me to close my ears.

A few minutes later Etta arrived with water and clean rags. She wiped the blood around the gash on the man's forehead and quieted him down, but only for a moment. When Etta touched the wound, he started yelling.

Minnie frowned and pointed to Leb and me, saying the word "children." He looked at us a moment, then Etta began to scrub. He thrashed his head, saying the English words again and again.

"Papa is on his way!" Ruth hollered as she returned. She was running, afraid she had already missed something.

Adar stood and teetered against the garden wall. " Ai! Ai!" she wailed, taking Leb from me and Ruth by the hand.

"I don't want to leave," Ruth complained, looking back over her shoulder as Adar dragged her away.

"Come, hold these." Minnie handed me the reins to the horse. She knelt down next to Etta and held the man's head so they could inspect the wound. She dabbed at the large gash, which we could see clearly once the blood was wiped away.

The man calmed down a little and began to speak. Minnie motioned with her hands for him to slow down. "Repeat, repeat," she kept saying.

I was pleased with myself for understanding the words "horse" and "trees," and when Papa came a few minutes later, I heard the whole story as Minnie translated it for him.

"The man is traveling to New Mexico," she said. "He has a camp not far from here." She paused and motioned to the place where the trail dropped into the first ravine. "This afternoon, he bought a horse from Mr. Black. On the way to his camp, a rattlesnake spooked the horse. It galloped into a thicket of trees, and that is the last thing he remembers until now."

I had been so busy watching the injured man, I had not looked closely at the horse. When I did, I could not believe my eyes. It was the horse from the hotel—the same horse that got me in trouble when Ruth wanted to ride, the one that took me on a wild-goose chase to the cemetery, then pretended to have been standing in front of the hotel all along. It was the horse with the white star on his face and the golden-brown eyes.

Now the horse was here. What trouble would he get me into now?

Minnie and Etta finished washing the man's wound, then wrapped it with clean strips of cloth. He smiled and made a joke as he tried to fit his hat back on over the bandages. A moment later he stood, shaking one leg, then the other, and rubbing the back of his neck. That was when I noticed he was wearing a gun strapped to the belt at his waist.

"Thank you," he said. He limped over to the horse and took the reins from me, then he knelt down to look at the horse's injured front leg.

I felt suddenly woozy. A long piece of flesh dangled from the horse's knee, and underneath it, bloody bone showed through. I stepped behind the man, but I could not take my eyes off the injured leg.

The man shook his head. He straightened up and removed the gun from his holster. He lifted it and pointed right at the white star on the horse's forehead.

"No! Stop!" I screamed. I pushed the man's arm upward. The gun fired, and the horse reared, pulling the man off his feet and dropping him down again. He plunged into me, and we both fell, scrambling in the dirt below the frightened horse.

"Gevalt! Gevalt! What has happened?" People came running from all directions. The man grabbed for the horse's reins and skidded along the ground a few feet to a stop. He steadied the horse and stood, with new scrapes and cuts on his elbows and arms.

I stood, too, and brushed off my skirt, looking back and forth from Papa to the man. They were both frowning at me.

"What crazy thing is this?" Etta scolded me. "You could have been shot!" She told the story, jabbering and pointing to the man and the horse. "And now I will have to wash and bandage his arms as well." She glared at me again.

My face turned scarlet. If there had been a place to hide, I would have run there quickly. The man with the gun towered above me, still holding the reins of the injured horse. We both stood staring at the circle of people around us. Even Adar had returned with Ruth and Leb to see what was the matter.

The man picked up his gun and shook his head, dumbfounded.

Finally Sarah Luper asked, "Why was he going to shoot the horse?"

"It has a bad leg," Isaac Kessel said, pointing. "A horse is no good with a bad leg."

"It is bad to lose a good horse just because of a bad leg."

"It is no good to lose a horse at all."

"It is worse to lose your head," Sarah said to finish it, and I did not know if she was talking about me or the man with the bandages. The man slipped the gun back into his holster and searched around for his hat, which had flown off his head in the scuffle.

"Perhaps he has lost his senses," Rachel Schloff said.

"Perhaps he had none to begin with."

"What do you expect from someone who has had two accidents in one day?" Etta said. "He's unlucky, this one."

"Yes, the man has no *mazel*."

"The horse has no *mazel*."

"The man and the horse have no *mazel*." Heads bobbed up and down in agreement.

Minnie walked over and picked up the man's hat. She handed it to him, and I could hear her speaking softly to him in English. Everyone stopped talking and leaned forward like bent trees.

The man stepped sideways, tightening his grip on the reins while Minnie knelt down and looked closely at the horse's injury. When she was finished, Minnie spoke with the man again in English, pointing to the bone and blood.

The man shook his head.

Minnie spoke again, pointing toward the mountains and the pasture where our milk cow grazed.

The man shrugged, dabbing at his bloody elbow with his shirtsleeve.

Minnie turned to Papa and spoke in Yiddish. "He says he does not want the horse. It is no good to him in this condition.

He has another horse in his camp, and he must leave tomorrow. If we want the horse, we can have it."

Papa wrinkled his brow. "What will we do with a horse that cannot walk?"

"In time, I think it will mend," Minnie said.

"We have enough work to do without caring for a crippled horse," Sarah complained.

A few heads nodded in agreement.

"I will take care of it," Minnie said. "Jonas and I worked with injured horses when we helped with the pack trains in Leadville."

Everyone looked around for Jonas. He stood quietly at the back of the group and nodded.

Suddenly a voice cried out, but I could have sworn it was not my own. "Papa, please. Please don't let the man shoot the horse. I will help Minnie take care of it. I know the horse will get better!"

Papa studied me for a long moment. Finally he said, "A lame horse is a burden. It will take much work, and if the leg does not heal ..."

"Please, Papa."

I thought I would die waiting for his answer. Under my breath, I practiced in English counting the number of times Papa stroked his beard.

"I will let you try, but—"

"Thank you, Papa!" I ran and threw my arms around him. "You will not be sorry. The horse will get better, and then we will have him to help with the work."

81

Etta snorted. "A girl's silliness should not be rewarded."

"A girl who almost got herself killed," added Sarah.

"I once knew a man with a three-legged horse … ," Isaac began.

Everyone groaned. It was a story they had heard over and over again. "We know. We know." Rachel shushed him with a wave.

People walked away, shaking their heads and muttering, "Meshuga, meshuga. Crazy, crazy. The horse will have to be shot in the end."

I swallowed hard. I did not mean to make them unhappy with me.

Only Papa, Minnie, and Jonas remained, standing in a small circle around the man and horse.

"Do you need a place to sleep tonight?" Papa asked. The man shook his head, pointing down the hill toward his camp.

"Then I will help you carry your things."

Jonas brought a coil of rope and looped it around the horse's neck. He held it tightly while the man removed the bridle and saddle. When the blanket came off, I saw an angel. All this time, I had thought the horse's coat was all brown, but underneath the saddle, white as snow, there it was—an angel with wings outstretched and ready to fly.

Papa threw the saddle over his shoulder and started with the man down the trail.

"Wait!" I called after them.

They stopped and turned.

"Does the horse have a name?"

Minnie translated, and the man laughed, then said, "His name is Lucky."

"Lucky?" I looked at Minnie to see what he meant.

"Mazel," she said. "That is why the man is laughing."

I reached over and stroked the angel on the horse's side. "Mazel. It is a good name for you."

I turned to wave to the man and felt something wet and rubbery on the back of my neck.

It was the soft, warm nose of the horse.

12

The worst was over—cutting the piece of dangling skin from Mazel's leg and wrapping a bandage around it. He did not like it when Minnie held his leg and Jonas cut through the loose flesh and cleaned the wound with something that made it sting. It was my job to hold the twitch—a rope tied tightly around his upper lip to keep him from moving around.

"If we don't do this, the leg will get infected," Minnie explained, "and then it will not heal."

I looked the other way and tried not to listen to the grating sound. Mazel tried to twist away, but I gave the twitch a turn so he would not move until the job was finished. His ears were laid back flat.

Mazel's ears are the secret to how he is feeling. When we were cleaning his leg, they lay down flat to show he was unhappy. But when I scratch him under the chin and talk to him, they prick forward and move around. I know he is listening to what I say.

It has been only three weeks, and already he knows me. He knows I am the one who saved him. Every day he walks over to sniff at my pocket to see if I have brought him something to eat, then he tickles my neck when he nuzzles me.

"You are my horse," I tell him. "I will always take care of you, and I will never let anything happen to you."

Papa would not want me thinking the horse is mine. I have tried to squash the thought like I do the cabbage worms that eat holes in the leaves of our plants, but like the cabbage worms, the thoughts keep coming back.

When I asked Minnie if it is wrong to want Mazel for myself, she did not scold me like Papa would have done, but said, "It is all right to have dreams. Dreams are like little seeds that, once planted, can grow into beautiful gardens."

It is Adar who wants to turn my dreams into nightmares. She does not like the horse and so makes sure I have little time to spend with it.

"Where are you going?" she asked today when I tried to slip out without her noticing. "And what is that you are spilling?" She picked up an oat flake and held it to the light. "It's coming from your pocket."

I grabbed my dress and pinched the pocket so no more oats would leak out. "It is for the horse." I could not think quickly enough to lie.

Adar narrowed her eyes at me. "You give good food to a horse and leave us to starve?"

My heart dropped into my stomach. "We are not starving," I said.

Adar tipped the canister that held our oats until the bottom showed. "This is all we have," she said, "and it must last until after the harvest."

"The harvest will be soon," I said. "We are near the end of summer."

Adar shook her head. "Everything is still small. Besides, you are wasting food on a horse that will have to be shot."

"Who says it will be shot?"

"Who is not saying it? People think Papa should get rid of it. It is foolish to keep a horse that does no work."

"When the horse gets better, they will not think it is foolish."

"That will be when gefilte fish leap from the frying pan," Adar said. "The horse is eating the grass we need for the milk cow. And it is eating our food, too. Papa will not like it when he finds out."

I could not hold back the words that flew from my mouth. "If you tell Papa about the oats, I will tell him that you have been making excuses to go and talk to Isaac Kessel."

Adar's face turned bright red. She did not know I had seen her walk out of her way to pass Isaac as he worked on the large root cellar at the end of the garden. She did not know I overheard him say how difficult it is to raise two daughters on his own.

"We can spare a few oats," Adar said quickly. "We will have money when our crops are harvested."

"The horse is getting better," I told her. "You should come see him."

"I have more important things to do than visit with a horse." She waved me away and went back to her work.

I ran all the way to the pasture, afraid that already Mazel would be gone. At first I did not see him, then he stepped out from the trees and trotted over, sniffing my dress pocket until I fed him the oats he knew I would bring.

I hugged his neck and whispered into his ear, "I won't let Papa shoot you. I won't. I won't!" A chilly wind caught the hem of my dress.

"I'm glad you are here." Minnie walked toward me with something looped over her arm. "I have a gift for Mazel," she said. "Jonas has been working on it in his spare time."

Minnie uncoiled a bridle that had been braided from strips of sacking. The bit had been made from a discarded wagon pin.

"Let's see if it fits." Minnie slipped the metal bar into Mazel's mouth and pulled the headpiece over his ears, cinching it tight. Mazel jumped sideways in surprise, shaking his head until Minnie pulled on the reins and brought him forward again. She stroked the side of his neck. "Soon he will be ready to ride."

"But he is still limping," I said.

"It is getting less. In a few more weeks he will be fine."

"I wish he would hurry. Everyone is saying he should be shot."

"There is a reason his name is Mazel." Minnie slipped the bridle from his head and coiled the reins into a large loop. "You need to be patient."

"I do not want to be patient," I said. "I want Mazel better. Now."

Minnie laughed at me.

Just then, the wind picked up a loose tumbleweed and blew it under Mazel's hoofs. He galloped away, kicking up his hind legs in a crooked sort of way because of his injury.

87

"The weather is changing," Minnie said. "It is Mazel's way of telling us."

I looked up at thick gray clouds rolling over the mountains. One of them was the face of a monster, opening its mouth wide to swallow the tops of the peaks.

"Adar says we are running out of food," I told Minnie. "We will have no more oats until we get paid for our harvest."

Minnie looked at the gathering clouds and frowned.

"Maybe I could bring him carrots from the garden."

"I don't think you'd better," Minnie said. "We will need all the food in the garden to make it through the winter."

"But after the harvest …"

"We will hope for a long fall," Minnie said. "With the planting so late, we will need extra weeks of growing time to make a good crop."

"How many more weeks?" I asked Minnie.

Another gust of wind hit us. The air felt cold and prickly. Minnie looked again at the mountain peaks and shook her head in a worried way. "Too many, I'm afraid."

A chilly shiver slid up my spine, and I thought about Mama's ring. What would happen if we did not have a good harvest and Papa could not get it back?

A week later, Ruth pulled the blanket from the window beside our bed and looked out. "The bushes are covered with white frosting."

I had been dreaming about Mazel loping through a field of wildflowers. He did not limp but moved gracefully, gathering speed until he launched into the sky, galloping into the chilly white clouds.

"It is not frosting," Adar said. "The bushes are covered with ice."

"Wake up! Wake up!" A pounding on the door shook our house, and I could not stay in my dream. Etta barged in without waiting for us to answer. "The garden has frosted! If we do not hurry, we will lose everything."

No more wildflowers or flying horses. My dream turned to a waking nightmare of picking peas and beans, pulling tomato vines, looking for cucumbers under frozen plants, and carrying squash to the root cellar, back and forth and back and forth. We did not stop to rest or eat but snacked on bread and cheese that tasted gritty because there was no time to wash our hands.

At dark we came inside. Ruth collapsed onto the bed next to Leb and fell asleep without even taking off her shoes.

Adar and I did not stop but snapped beans and peeled beets, dropping them into jars and sealing them with a boiling water bath while Papa continued to bring in more food by lantern light.

When the last quart was placed into the canning pot, I lay my head on the table, listening to the jars jiggle-joggle gently as they tapped the sides of the kettle. The wind whistled outside, and a strong blast blew the blankets that covered our windows. Adar hurried to tack them down as Papa came in and sank into the chair next to me.

"It's snowing."

"We should not be having bad weather so soon," Adar said. "It's so early."

"Too early," Papa replied.

Those are the last words I remember before climbing into bed and slipping off to sleep. I dreamed again of Mazel. Only this time, I could not find him. Snow swirled everywhere, covering Mazel's hoofprints, which led away in a dark frozen line.

I followed his tracks until I came to a clearing in the trees, where Mazel stood looking at Mama's ring. It hung above him on the branch of a tall pine, dangling just out of my grasp. I stretched up for it, reaching as far as I could, but each time I brushed it with my fingertips, it moved away from me, floating farther and farther until it drifted up into the sky.

Mazel swooped me up and we flew after it, dipping and spinning and diving. Each time we passed it, I leaned farther out, stretching … stretching. Finally I grabbed for the ring, clasping it tightly in my fist, but as I did, I fell, tumbling over and over in the dark until I landed in the snow outside our house.

When I opened my hand, it was empty. Mama's ring was gone.

My dream woke me. I shivered and pulled on the covers. Adar tugged back, squeezing Ruth between us.

A cold wind blew through the blankets that covered our windows, and I could not get warm. I thought about Mama's ring, wrapped in velvet cloth inside Mr. Black's cash register. Now that our crops had frosted, we would never see it again.

"I don't like Papa leaving us," Ruth said.

"It is only during the day," Adar soothed, placing the challah bread in the center of the table next to the Sabbath candle.

"But he is far away."

"He is near Cotopaxi," Adar explained. Ruth could not understand why Papa and the other men had had to take jobs away from home. "He will be here tonight."

"He is in a hole all day," Ruth said, "where it is dark."

"A mine," Adar corrected her.

"A mine is a big hole in the ground," Ruth insisted.

I tried not to think about Papa working underground, where water drips through small cracks in the earth and the sun does not shine. I did not tell Ruth that Etta said sometimes there are cave-ins and people get buried alive.

"Papa will be home soon," I said.

Adar paced back and forth, lifting a blanket that hung over one of the windows to keep out the cold, then dropping it back down. Leb sat on the bed, playing with two spoons. He banged them together and babbled until Adar snatched them away, then walked back and forth some more.

"It is getting dark," Ruth said. "Will we be able to have the Sabbath without Papa?"

"The Sabbath comes by itself," Adar sighed, dropping the spoons into the dishpan. She took one last look out the window and picked up little Leb, handing him to me as we sat down at the table. Slowly she lit the candle. Ruth and I waited and waited for Adar to begin the prayers, but she did not. We stared at the candle in silence with our ears turned toward the door.

Finally we heard footsteps, and Papa came in. His face was so black, you could not tell where his beard stopped and his cheeks began. He dropped into his chair at the table.

Adar shrieked, "Papa! You must wash." She jumped up for the pan of warm water she had prepared for him earlier and brought it over. After he washed, the water was not even fit to scrub our floor.

After dinner, Ruth asked Papa, "Will you tell us a story?"

Always, this is when Papa smiles and puts Leb on one knee and Ruth on the other and starts a tale about the Bal Shem Tov, the magical rabbi. This time Papa shook his head and removed his boots, one heavy foot at a time.

Even Leb could not cheer him. He crawled up on Papa's lap and pulled on his beard, making his own hands black from touching the places Papa did not get clean.

Finally Papa asked about our day. Ruth burst into tears and showed him her hands that were red and scraped from helping Etta pull the last of the turnips from the garden.

"Hush," Adar scolded her. "Papa has enough to worry about without looking at your fingers."

I wanted to tell Papa about the root cellar—about how it was still not full even with the turnips and other root vegetables added. I bit my lip, thinking about how we walked through the garden, turning over dry vines to make sure we had not missed anything. The cabbages Ruth and I had worked so hard to save from the worms were only a little larger than Papa's fist.

"Papa, will we be able to plant more food?" Ruth asked. "The weather is better now."

"You cannot plant in the fall," I told her. "Things will not grow."

"Then how will we eat?" Ruth asked. "Etta said there will not be enough for the winter."

"Shhhhh!" Adar said.

I could not help but think about the small carrot I found when we combed through the garden one last time. I pulled it and put it in my pocket to take to Mazel. I should not have been so selfish. Now, when I see Papa already asleep on his cot, I feel bad about it. I should have saved it for him.

13

I heard little Leb's cries from the creek and ran to the house as fast as I could, sloshing water from the buckets onto the skirt of my dress.

"I thought you were watching him!" Adar said. She was bouncing Leb to stop him from crying.

I put down my pails and looked at the boards from the unfinished shutters on the ground below our windows. Papa had been working on them in his spare time, and a sharp nail poked upward through one of the boards.

"I was bringing the water," I told Adar.

"You should have let me know." Adar used her apron to dab at a scrape above Leb's eye, where a bump was beginning to rise. "Bring me a cloth and some soap."

Ruth scampered into the house and came back with a clean cloth. Adar knelt down and dipped it into the cold water and washed his head, still cooing and trying to calm him.

"I don't know why he still cries." Her voice sounded edgy.

Then we saw the rip in Leb's pants. Underneath, Leb's skin was punctured. "It is from the nail," I said, pointing.

"It is only a small hole," Ruth said.

Adar frowned and took a closer look. "It would be better if he had no hole at all." She pinched around the wound to make it bleed, then scrubbed it hard. Leb began a new round of screaming.

"Will we have to shoot him?" Ruth asked.

Adar scowled at Ruth and lifted Leb back to her hip. "He is walking and climbing everywhere now," she said. "It is impossible to keep track of him by myself." She glared at me.

"He was in the house on the bed when I left," I said, wondering how the accident could have happened. Then I understood. The blankets Adar had been using to cover the windows were rolled up to let in the morning sun. Leb had pulled himself onto a windowsill and toppled out.

"I can take him now," I said, feeling terrible about the accident.

"It is now you think of helping?" Adar handed him to me and went back inside.

I joggled Leb a few more minutes, looking down at the unfinished shutter, thinking how Papa had helped everyone else first before finishing ours.

"We will go see Mazel," I told Leb. "He will cheer us both up."

With Leb on my hip, I started along the trail to the pasture. The rocks along the path sparkled in the September sun. "September." It was the new word I had learned for the month we call Tishri.

After the frost, the weather had warmed. Even the snow on the mountains had melted away, leaving the peaks barren and gray. The remaining grass in the pasture waved its seeded shoots in the morning breeze.

Mazel stood under a tree at the upper end of the pasture. At first he did not see us, then he looked up and trotted over, sniffing for a handful of oats or a bit of something from the garden.

"Not today," I told him. "We have no more oats until Papa earns more credit at the store."

Mazel turned his ears toward me as if listening to every word, then he nosed Leb curiously. Leb pulled back and let out a little squeal, then he leaned forward, reaching for Mazel's face. I held him closer so he could touch Mazel's cheek.

"Horse," I said to Leb in English.

"Hohsh," Leb said in baby talk.

"You will be speaking English before I do," I told him. He reached for Mazel again, grabbing the hair of his mane and giving it a hard pull. Mazel did not like this and stepped out of reach, twitching his ears.

"Hohshy," Leb said again, pointing.

The way he said it made me laugh, and Leb laughed, too. I was glad that I was able to cheer him up and make him forget about his fall. When I turned back toward the house, I saw Minnie coming through the gate, pushing the cow back to the pasture after its morning milking. She waved at me as she passed Mazel's bridle hanging on the post near the gate.

"Do you think we can give little Leb a ride?" I asked.

Minnie came over to look at Mazel's injured leg. "He is still limping a little, but Leb is so light, I don't think Mazel will notice."

We put on the bridle, and I lifted Leb onto Mazel's back. I steadied him there and walked beside him while Minnie slowly led the horse around the pasture. Leb grabbed onto the long mane and bobbed up and down above the angel wings on Mazel's side. He made little chuckling noises, almost as if he were saying, *Look at me. I am up here floating with the seraphim.*

When it was time to go back to the house, Leb did not want to leave. He reached for Mazel, spreading his pudgy fingers, then curling them around the horse's mane. "Hohshy," he said.

"I will bring you back," I promised Leb. "And when Papa sees you riding Mazel, he will not ever think about shooting him."

When Papa came home, he did not scold us about Leb's accident, but he went outside after he had eaten and finished building our shutters by lamplight. I fell asleep listening to the pounding of Papa's hammer. The sound made me dream of the vendor who sold apples from a cart near our house in Kishinev.

The vendor passed by our house, and we could hear the Tsar's soldiers arguing with him.

"I cannot give these away," the vendor said. "I have worked hard to grow them, and I need the money for my family."

There was a loud crash, and we looked out our window to see the soldiers overturning the cart and smashing it with their clubs. Red apples spilled like blood onto the road.

"Papa, come quick!" I yelled.

Papa stopped his lessons and ran outside, shouting, "No!

No!" The soldiers just laughed at him, climbed on their horses, and rode away, pockets filled with fresh fruit.

Papa sent his students for nails and a hammer to repair the broken cart.

"The next time they come, I will let the soldiers have some," the vendor said, picking through the spilled apples to find the ones that were still good enough to sell.

"It's not right," Papa said.

"True." The vendor gave Papa a sackful of bruised apples. "But …" He shrugged as if to say there was nothing he could do about it.

The vendor did not seem like an old man to me, but when I watched him roll his cart away, his shoulders were bent over like the branches of an old willow tree.

Later Papa told Mama, "Perhaps it is better to starve in America than to starve here."

My dream stopped in the middle of the night when I heard Papa come inside. In the morning, the new shutters hung from their hinges, and the warmth from the stove filled our house. Papa was already gone.

I went to the creek for water. The grass and bushes were dewy, and the sun peeked over the horizon, making everything glisten. I made plans to take little Leb back up to the pasture to ride Mazel.

When I returned to the house, Adar was changing Leb's wrapper. "You need to go see Etta to get some medicine for Leb's leg," she said.

I looked at the place where the nail had gone in and could

see that it was turning red. I hurried to Etta's and returned with a jar of salve. When we rubbed it on his leg he fussed a little, but Ruth tickled him until he cheered up.

"I can take him for a while," I said to Adar. "It will do him good to be outside."

Adar shook her head. "I need you and Ruth to collect fresh grass for our mattress. It is as flat as a griddle, and it needs to be done before it snows again."

"It won't snow today," I said. "The sun is shining."

"All the better reason for you to go today."

Mazel trotted over to the pasture fence and whinnied at us as we passed by. "Tomorrow," I said to him. "Tomorrow I will bring Leb back for another ride."

When we returned and refilled the mattress, Ruth jumped up on it, rolling back and forth like a rolling pin to flatten the lumps. Adar put little Leb next to Ruth and bounced him, but he did not smile and roll around the way he usually did.

"Maybe he is sick," I said. "Maybe we should tell Papa about it when he gets home."

"Papa is not coming home tonight," Adar said. "Remember, he is going to work the night shift at the mine. It will earn extra money."

Leb began to whimper, and I picked him up. He felt hot, and when I pulled back his clothing to look at his leg, it was fiery red with streaks that looked like a spider's web going away from the hole where the nail had gone in.

That night, as soon as we climbed into bed, Leb began to cry. First Adar, then me, and then Ruth took turns walking around the house, holding and rocking and hugging him. Nothing would comfort him.

Ruth finally dropped into bed and fell asleep, then Adar lay down and closed her eyes, saying, "I will rest only a few minutes."

I sat down in a chair by the stove, too tired to move anymore. I hummed to Leb, a melody Mama used to hum. Finally, it soothed him to sleep.

14

In my mind I keep seeing Leb sitting on Mazel's back on top of the angel's wings. He is laughing. I did not realize that it would be the last time I would ever hear him laugh.

Papa was holding Leb when he died, and I cannot bear to think about the look on his face. The man in the chair did not look like Papa. He looked like a stone statue staring at nothing.

At first I thought Papa was just tired after sitting up all night, but when I opened the shutters to let in the sun, he shook his head and asked me to close them. I noticed, then, that Leb was not breathing. I don't know how long Papa had been sitting like that. It looked like years and years.

When Adar woke up and saw what had happened, she screamed and pulled at the collar of her nightdress, ripping it diagonally across her heart. I reached up to do the same, but Papa held up his free hand to stop me. "It will not be soon that we can replace your clothing," he said quietly. "God can read your heart and knows it has been torn apart."

I do not know what came over me, but I ran from the house without shoes or stockings. I had no coat and was not fully dressed. I did not feel the sharp rocks cutting my feet or the cold bite of the morning air. I ran until I found Mazel and threw my arms around his neck, burying my face in his thick brown mane.

Later Etta came for me and told me it was time to go back inside. "It is not proper for you to be here once the mourning has begun."

I could not feel the tiny cuts in my bare feet. I felt heavy like the granite of the mountains that towered above us. "It is your fault!" I shouted at the mountains. "This would never have happened if we had not come to this terrible place in this terrible, terrible country!"

The mountains did not answer but stood dark and uncaring like the Tsar's soldiers. *We are here and will always be here,* the soldiers jeered at me. *You cannot run from us. We are everywhere, haunting you.*

I walked back to the house, unable to feel even the cold air on my skin.

It took a few minutes for my eyes to adjust to the dim light inside. The shutters were closed, with only narrow slivers of light leaking in around the edges. Another thin rim of light framed the door, and a halo surrounded our stovepipe where it passed through the roof.

I did not want to think about the days of mourning when we would be shut inside. When Mama died, we had more space to move around. When Mama died, we had little Leb to think about …

I looked once more at the closed shutters. If only they had been finished the day Leb fell out. If only we had real windows instead of windows of air. If only I had come back from the creek with the water a minute earlier. If only …

Leb lay on the table, wrapped in a blanket. I did not want to believe it was him, and I willed myself to walk over and touch the skin of his cheek. It felt cold and waxy. The truth came through my fingers. Leb was gone.

I tried not to cry, but a tear slipped down my cheek, then another and another. I could not hold them back.

Visitors came, prayed, and left quietly, opening and closing the door to let in the daylight that flickered and disappeared again. It was the only daylight we saw until we left on the long walk to Cotopaxi, where Mr. Stokes and Isaac Kessel had dug a small grave for Leb in the cemetery on the hill above the hotel.

They set it apart from the other graves in a corner by itself, but still, from where I stood, I could see the markers of strangers scattered between rocks and dry patches of grass. I did not want to leave Leb alone on that hill. We did not know these people. No one here would watch out for Leb.

"Blessed be the righteous judge." I heard a ripping sound as Adar rent her dress.

"Blessed be the righteous judge." This time Papa did not stop me. I reached up with shaky hands and took hold of my dress and pulled at my collar until the cloth gave way.

I cannot think how God in his righteousness could take little Leb away. Leb is the last thing in this world that Mama left us, and now he, too, is gone. The hole in my heart will never mend.

15

The leaves on the willows along the creek have yellowed and started to fall to the ground like teardrops. September is gone. Rosh Hashanah and now Yom Kippur have passed.

It is the sound of the shofar that haunts me. At night, when I try to sleep, all I can hear are the ghostlike echoes blowing through the hollow of the curved ram's horn. The long, mournful tone does not stop but continues to wail, keeping me awake until the light comes through the cracks in our shutters. Finally I doze until it is time to get up for chores.

I am wishing now that the ram's horn had been lost on our journey across the Atlantic. Saul Borsten carried it like a baby, wrapped in a velvet cloth. He never put it with our other luggage and never let it out of his sight.

Now at night, all I can think about is the way it sounded when he blew it at the end of our Yom Kippur service. At first a long, low single note. Then the weeping … the broken notes … the longer pulsing that sounds like human crying.

When I try to sleep, these sounds come and go, but it is the drawn-out note at the end that won't leave me. It lingers, the final mournful tone fading, but never disappearing.

Mama, Mama, Mama. Leb, Leb. It is a long, sad song that will never end.

Even when Minnie comes to see me, I do not want to talk to her. For two weeks now, she has been trying.

"You must come with me to Etta's to practice your English," she says. "If you don't, you will forget everything you have learned."

Already the words are gone from my mind. What difference does it make? I will not go out. I will stay here in the house until I am old with wrinkly skin and all my teeth are falling out. Things are not the same. They will never be the same again.

Minnie finally insisted. She would not leave our door until I agreed to go with her. On the way to Etta's house she asked, "Have you been to the pasture to see Mazel?"

"I have been busy," I said, looking at the little shed attached to Etta's house where the chickens were kept.

"Busy brooding," Minnie said. "You are worse than an old hen."

I glanced at the autumn sunset, not wanting to meet her eyes. The days were getting shorter, and soon it would be dark. It did not seem fair that summer was already gone and fall was here. It ended too soon. Everything ended too soon. … Once again I heard the sound of the ram's horn.

"It is not for me," Minnie said, interrupting my thoughts. "It is Mazel. When I go to the pasture to check on him, he does not trot over, only stands and looks at me from a distance. He misses you."

"He is lame," I said. "Papa will shoot him and then …" I could not finish. All I could think about was losing Mama and now little Leb. *It is better to ignore Mazel*, I thought, *to pretend he isn't there.* I could not bear to lose him, too.

"He is better," Minnie said. "You must come and see."

"Not today," I told her.

"Tomorrow, then." The look on Minnie's face told me she would not let me say no. "I will come for you in the morning."

In the morning, I put on my sweater and followed Minnie outside. The blue sky framed the Blood of Christ Mountains, and a warm breeze tickled my cheeks.

"I don't know why God brought the frost to kill our garden, then turned around and made things warm again," I said.

"In America they call this weather Indian summer."

The woman with the round stomach and the scar on her face came into my mind. "If this is Indian summer, what makes an Indian winter?"

"Cold," Minnie said.

We reached the pasture. Mazel's bridle still hung from the fence post where we left it the day I took little Leb for a ride. I remembered Leb pointing with his pudgy finger and saying "hohsh." I pushed the thought from my mind.

"I'll wait for you here," Minnie said, leaning on the top rail of the fence.

Mazel stood in the center of the pasture with his tail swishing as he ate. As I approached, he pricked his ears and turned so I could see fully the angel's wings on his side. Then he turned his back on me and continued eating as if nothing out of the ordinary had happened.

My heart fell. He did not know me and did not even want to see me. With tears in my eyes I started back across the pasture, listening to the brittle yellow grass crackle under my step. *One by one*, I thought, *the things I love are disappearing, like the leaves on the willows along the creek.*

And then I heard hoofbeats behind me. Thud- thud … thud-thud, then a tickle on the back of my neck. Horse lips. Mazel nudged me, nibbling down to the pocket where I used to carry oats.

I whirled and buried my face in his mane. "Mazel! Mazel! You have not forgotten me!"

Surprised, Mazel jumped and trotted away a few steps. I noticed then that he no longer had a limp, and the hair on his leg had grown back.

"You were right!" I shouted to Minnie. "He is better!" I caught Mazel and stroked his neck. "You are better, *bubeleh*! Now Papa will want to keep you forever and ever."

Minnie walked across the pasture, carrying Mazel's bridle.

"Mazel is much thinner," I said.

Minnie laughed. "We are all thinner." She slipped the bridle over his head and adjusted it to fit. "Would you like to ride him?"

I shook my head, looking around to make sure no one was watching. "Papa would not like it."

Minnie stood for a long moment, holding the reins and looking at the Blood of Christ Mountains. "I will not tell you to go against your papa's wishes," she said. "You must think it over and decide for yourself."

I brushed Mazel's mane, remembering the day in Cotopaxi when Ruth wanted to ride, and the day Mazel galloped to the cemetery. Already I had displeased Papa so many times. What if he would not forgive me?

Then I thought about Minnie coming to America to marry Jonas. She had displeased her papa, and still he had forgiven her.

In the end, it was Mazel who made up my mind. He danced away, pulling on the reins as if to say, *I do not want to stand here all day. Let's go.* Like the white angel on his side, he wanted to fly.

"I will try," I said.

"You will do fine."

Minnie led Mazel to a fallen tree. She steadied him while I used the stump for a step and swung up onto Mazel's back. I held tightly to his mane and straightened up slowly, trying to keep from slipping off sideways.

From my perch, I looked around at the pasture … at the cow chewing her cud and the little mounds of earth where small animals burrowed. I wanted to take off and fly like the Bal Shem Tov for a magical ride.

"Don't try to go too fast at first," Minnie warned as she handed me the reins. "Nudge him in the sides with your legs to make him move."

I pressed and nothing happened. All my thoughts of flying vanished.

"A little more," Minnie encouraged me.

I prodded him again, this time too much. Mazel leapt forward, throwing me backward. When I pulled the reins to catch myself, he jerked to a halt. I lurched forward, dropping the reins and grabbing on to his mane to keep from falling off.

Minnie laughed, picking up the reins and handing them to me. "It would be easier with a saddle," she said, "but we will have to make do."

I thought, then, that I should get off and stop trying. All I could think about was the gossip about the woman at Mr. Black's store.

"She is riding like a man," Etta snorted. "And wearing pants!"

"These American women have no manners," Sarah agreed.

"No decency."

"No self-respect."

Minnie interrupted my thoughts. "You will get better with practice," she said. "Ride him around the pasture."

I kicked Mazel lightly. This time, he moved forward with ease. I walked him around and came back to the stump, feeling proud of myself. "Can I ride him another day?" I asked, sliding down to the ground.

"Yes, as long as you make sure your work is finished and you do not get in trouble with Adar."

Minnie showed me how to take the bridle off and put it on again until I could do it by myself. When we were finished, Mazel followed us to the gate, and I patted him on the neck. "I'll come back tomorrow," I told him.

We hung the bridle on the post so I would know where to find it, and I kept my promise to Mazel, coming whenever I could to ride him.

16

I have not been this frightened since little Leb was sick. Last night we stayed outside, feeding wood to a huge fire to keep the bears away. We have seen three of them near our houses, and there are tracks every day along the creek.

"It is not enough that they have gotten in the cellar to eat our cabbages," Etta said, "but there are claw marks on the door to our chicken shed."

The fire crackled and a spray of orange sparks flew up. "We will have to move the chickens inside our own houses to keep them safe," Sarah said.

"If there are any left." The frown on Etta's face looked eerie in the glow of the firelight.

Ruth pulled on my sleeve and whispered, "Papa told me the bears go to sleep for the winter."

"It is the weather," I told her. "The warm temperature is keeping them awake."

"When will Papa and the others be back?"

"Soon," I said, hoping that Papa and the men would not see any bears as they walked home from Cotopaxi.

"Does Papa have his gun?"

I thought about Papa's gun, and I remembered him telling Benjamin, "I might as well drop it in the creek. I have no more ammunition, and none can be bought for it here in America."

"Will a bear eat people?" Ruth asked.

"Not if we stay close to the fire." But I was worrying about Mazel being up in the pasture, wondering if he would be all right.

Just then, I heard a shrill squeal and a wild neighing, high-pitched and terrible. I raced from the fire and ran without stopping until I reached the pasture gate. I stood there for a moment, heart pounding, squinting into the blackness of the night.

Only my own loud breathing broke the silence.

Then, at the upper end of the pasture, a dark prowling shadow passed between the trees.

"Mazel, is that you?"

No answer.

Knees quivering, I slipped through the gate into the pasture. If it was a bear, what would keep it from eating *me*?

Again I heard an animal cry. This time a loud bellow, hoofbeats, and another wild squeal. Thinking only of my Mazel, I raced across the pasture, afraid of what I would find.

Later they told me my scream echoed for miles. It was heard by Papa and the other men as they hiked up the trail from Cotopaxi and by everyone at the fire.

All I can remember is running through the dark until I came close enough to see Mazel rearing up on his hind legs as the bear swiped the air with its powerful front paws. I tripped over something on the ground, and when I stood up my hands were covered with blood.

That is when I fainted.

When I opened my eyes, I saw a circle of light made by burning lamps. At first I thought it was the glowing lights of heaven, but when I looked for Mama, she was not there. The smell of sage woke me. My head throbbed and everything blurred.

"Is she alive?" I heard Ruth say.

"Oy." Adar was kneeling beside me, fanning me with the hem of her skirt. "What could you have been thinking?"

I sat up slowly and looked around at the faces of Minnie, Ruth, and Adar. Close by, a group of people hovered over the bleeding milk cow. "Bring my sewing basket," Etta called.

Sarah and Rachel started off across the pasture huddled beneath the fingernail moon. A few minutes later they returned with the sewing basket. Along with them came Papa and the other men.

Everyone began talking at once, telling the story of the marauding bears. "And now this," Etta said, pointing to the bleeding cow. "Why couldn't it have been that worthless horse that gives us no milk?"

It came back to me, then. The bear's sharp claws, and Mazel's front hooves flashing. "Mazel reared up and frightened the bear away," I said.

"It could not be," Etta said. "You are but a foolish girl that runs into the night without thinking first."

"Mazel protected the cow. I saw it happen."

Papa frowned at me. "You were out here alone?"

"The horse ... it cried for me."

Minnie held the lamp for Etta as she threaded a large needle. Two men knelt on the cow's neck and two held her hind legs while Etta jabbed the needle through the cow's thick hide, making the first stitch. The cow let out a long, low moan.

"It will be a miracle if she survives," Etta said when she had finished.

The men released the cow and backed away. She stood up on wobbly legs.

"We must walk her close to the house where she will be safe." Everyone agreed and turned to go.

"Papa," I said. "Can I bring Mazel, too?"

Papa sighed. "You can bring Mazel, too."

Mazel followed us to the gate, where I found his bridle and put it on. On the outskirts of the fire, I tied his reins to a low bush and stroked his mane. "You will be safe here," I told him. "Until the bears go away."

That is when I heard Sarah Luper cry out. "The chickens, the chickens!" she shouted. "They are gone!"

We ran to the shed and found it smashed and splintered. Blood and feathers covered the floor.

"Over here," Benjamin called. The light from his lamp reflected up onto the roof of his house, where several chickens had fluttered to safety.

No one slept in their houses. We stayed awake, watching the little cinders from the fire flicker and float up to the stars.

Finally I drifted off with Ruth curled beside me. My dreams were of being chased by wild animals with large teeth and sharp claws. Mazel reared and screamed, but the wild animals kept coming.

17

The weather has finally changed, and now, instead of bears, we have winter pawing at our door. A week after our large campfire, in the middle of the night, I woke up to the drip, drop, sizzle of water seeping through the roof near our stovepipe. The droplets slid down the pipe and splattered on the hot surface, hissing and spitting.

Snow. Not just a little, but white everywhere. It blocked our door, and Papa had to scoop it away before he went out with his ax to find firewood.

"Soon it will be taller than little Leb." Ruth gasped and slapped her fingers to her lips, realizing what she had said.

"Hurry with the water," Adar told me. "The kettle on the stove is empty."

I buttoned my coat and stepped outside into the whirling flakes. I could not walk without lifting my feet high and dragging my dress in the snow. By the time I returned to the house, it felt as if I were pulling stones behind me.

"Look at what you've done to Etta's shoes," Adar said when I returned. Never mind my wet dress and frozen fingers. "You should have wrapped them in grain sacks before you went out."

I put down the full buckets and stood at the stove to warm my hands. Melting ice dripped from the hem of my dress.

"And we need eggs, too," Adar said. "Go see if Etta has any."

This time I took two grain sacks and wrapped them around my feet, tying them with twine. I made flat, floppy tracks all the way to Etta's house.

I knocked and waited. Inside I could hear Etta and Benjamin talking. "It is a miracle the cow is still alive." There was worry in Etta's voice. "And how will we feed her with all this snow?"

"We will find a way," Benjamin answered. "There are people who will sell us hay."

"And how will we pay?"

"Our new jobs with the railroad start tomorrow," he reminded her. "The pay is better."

"The jobs could not come at a worse time," Etta moaned. "For days now, we will be up here alone in the cold."

"God will help us through it," Benjamin said firmly. "He has not sent us here to starve."

"I am not worried about starving, but about freezing to death." I heard plates and silverware gathered roughly, clanking loudly into the dishpan. The iron door of the stove squeaked open and slammed shut again.

"We will not have to work on the Sabbath," Benjamin pressed. "This job is a gift."

"A whole week with the men away. It is a curse."

116

I was trying to imagine a week at a time without Papa when Benjamin added, "You can be thankful the bears have gone to hibernate."

"Soon we will have nothing left for the bears to eat but our own skin and bones," Etta said angrily. I raised my hand to knock again. "We should sell the horse. It does us no good, and still we must feed it." My hand did not move, but hung, midair.

"It frightened the bear away from our milk cow," Benjamin said.

"You believe that story?"

"The cow survived."

"And so now they can starve together."

At that moment, Benjamin opened the door. I blinked at him, trying to remember why I had come. "Eggs," I finally said. "Adar sent me for eggs."

"The chickens have slowed down their laying," Etta called over Benjamin's shoulder. "Later I can bring her some from the ones I have packed in salt."

Even following my tracks, I had trouble walking back to our house through the heavy snow. I gave Adar the message, and when she was not looking, took a small handful of oats from our new supply. I trudged up to the pasture and looked over the fence at Mazel as he pawed the ground for stems of dry grass to eat. I called to him and held out the oats. "You can have my share," I promised. "I will eat less."

Mazel nibbled from my hand, and when I drew it away, my fingers felt like frozen sticks.

"Maybe I can bring you something else after Papa gets his

117

railroad job." Mazel tipped his ears forward to listen. "He will be gone all week, but with the money, he can buy you some hay…."

I tried to make myself feel better about Papa's new job, wondering why Adar had not told me. When I returned to the house, I found out why. Adar did not know.

"A week? Where will they be?" Adar asked Etta. They sat at the table with the eggs between them.

"In the mountains," Etta said. "The railroad needs workers to cut trees for the new track beyond Salida."

"Salida!" Adar said. "It is a whole day from here."

"That is why they cannot come home at night. They will take the train from Cotopaxi and return each week for the Sabbath."

Adar held her head in her hands and moaned. "And if the snow continues, what then?"

Etta frowned and shook her head without answering. Adar looked up and saw me. "Where have you been?"

"Nowhere," I said.

"You cannot be 'nowhere.'" She narrowed her eyes, then studied my coat pocket. "It is the horse. You have been feeding him again."

"No," I lied, but she did not believe me.

"The horse, the horse," Etta said. "All we need is another mouth to feed." She threw up her hands and left our house.

"The horse needs to eat, too," Ruth said, taking my side. "It is cold outside, and he will starve."

"You should mind your own business," Adar snapped.

Ruth plunked down on the bed and pouted. In a minute a

tear slid down her cheek. "What will we do with Papa gone?" she finally said.

"He will be back every week for the Sabbath," I told her. Still Ruth did not cheer up until I offered to help her make a new doll from our old scraps of cloth.

"Can we find some yarn for her hair?" she asked.

"I can do better than that. I can cut a little hair from Mazel's tail and mane and we can sew it on."

The hair, as it turns out, has been a better idea than I first thought. When I want to visit Mazel, I tell Adar I need to go clip a little more hair for Ruth's doll. I tell her the pieces we have are too short or too stiff or won't stay on. It is not really a lie. Mazel's hair is not easy to work with. Still, I could get enough in one trip if I chose to.

Adar does not seem to notice that the doll is almost finished, and she does not notice that in the mornings, while she is busy straightening our blankets, I put a few oats in my coat pocket so they will be there when I am ready to go out.

It is Mazel and Ruth's doll that help the days pass quickly while we wait for Papa to come home. During the daytime, I do not miss Papa so much, but the dark nights last forever.

The first week Papa was gone, a scratching and chewing sound woke me up. I shook Adar. "Can you hear that?" I asked.

Adar rolled over. "It is outside," she said. "Go back to sleep."

I did not think it was outside. It was inside, I knew it, coming from the corner behind the stove.

Quietly I tiptoed over to the stove. It glowed dimly where light from the glimmering coals came through the cracks. I slipped behind it and stopped.

The chewing sound stopped.

I waited, and the sound began once more only to stop as I moved closer.

Suddenly a creature sprang out and ran across my bare toes and up my leg. I screamed, and the thing ran back down my leg, scampering across the cabin floor underneath our bed.

Adar flew from bed and lit the lamp. She began to scream, too, as a large furry shape flicked the hem of her nightdress and ran under the table.

By then Ruth was awake. She stood on the bed, crying, "I see it! I see it! It's an enormous rat!"

She pointed toward the corner near the door, where two round eyes stared at us, hypnotized by the bright lamp.

"Get the broom," Adar said. She bent forward, stretching out with the lamp, but keeping her bare feet back as far as she could.

"I'll hold the lamp," I said.

Adar moved the lamp out of my reach and gripped it more tightly. "*I'll* hold it."

"Let me get it," Ruth said, surprising us both. She popped off the bed, retrieved the broom, and headed for the corner, where she swung the broom over her head and brought it down with a loud *thwack*.

I did not know pack rats could jump, but this one did—almost to our door latch. Adar jumped back as the rat scrambled across the room, retreating to the corner behind the stove.

Ruth took off again, swinging the broom. I took the lamp from Adar and followed. *Thwack! Thwack!*

Just as the rat reached the place where I had first heard the gnawing, it disappeared into a crack between the wall and the cabin floor. The last thing we saw was its thin, scaly tale disappearing as Ruth smacked at it one last time.

"It was only a rat," she said matter-of-factly.

"A huge rat," Adar said, as if trying to explain why she had screamed. "Much bigger than Russian rats!"

I did not think so, but at home we did not have to worry about what would come into our house in the middle of the night without Papa there.

18

Already four candles are lit on our menorah, plus the shammes in the middle. It makes me think of Mama and her four children. Four, if you count Leb. I still do not believe that Leb is not here. Only a year ago, when we packed, it was my job to keep him from crawling into the piles of things we had stacked on the floor. Three piles: one to take to America, one to give away, and a pile we could not decide upon.

"We still have too much to carry," Papa said, looking from one pile to the next.

Adar sorted her clothes again. She had already given the ones that were too small to me. Another pile held Mama's old clothes, the ones Adar could adjust and wear. When she found Mama's wedding dress, she held it up and twirled in front of the mirror that leaned on the wall by the giveaway pile. She looked hopefully at Papa.

Papa studied Adar and the dress for a long moment, then sighed and shook his head. "We must leave it."

Adar dropped the dress into the giveaway pile and turned away with a heavy sigh.

"What about this?" Ruth asked, holding up the menorah that held our Hanukkah candles.

Papa looked from Ruth to the opened *pekel* that held our kiddush cups and silverware. "It is heavy," he said. "Perhaps it should be left."

"I will carry the *pekel*," I said. "It will not be too heavy for me."

"No," Papa said firmly. "We must draw the line somewhere."

Ruth put the menorah in with the giveaways, but when Papa turned his back, I retrieved it and wrapped it in one of my dresses. Papa did not find out about it until we reached New York City. In our hotel room, when we unpacked, it tumbled out, clanking when it hit the floor.

"What is this?" Papa's frown told me he already knew the answer to the question.

"I could not bear to leave it," I said.

Papa picked up the menorah and packed it in the *pekel* with our kiddush cups and silverware. When it was time to leave our hotel, he handed the *pekel* to me and said, "I know you will take care of this. It holds everything dear to us."

If I had known then that the *pekel* would break open and spill onto the railroad track at Cotopaxi, I would have begged Papa not to trust me with it. If I could live that moment again, I would get off the train gracefully and hold the bundle tightly. Then Mama's picture would not be in two pieces. If only putting things back together were as easy as breaking them apart.

A quiet knocking at our door kept me from going to look for the torn picture of Mama, which I keep hidden at the

123

bottom of our trunk. Adar quickly straightened her apron and tucked a stray hair behind her ear. Papa looked up from his reading. The candle flames flickered as Ruth opened the door.

Isaac Kessel stood there holding his hat in his hands. His two small daughters peeked out from behind his legs. "May I come in?"

Adar looked anxiously at Papa, who smiled. "Visitors are always welcome."

Ruth took Isaac's small daughters under her wing and showed them her new doll. The older girl, Miriam, two years younger than Ruth, sat on the bed next to her. The younger girl, Chava, stood quietly watching.

For a long while Isaac sat at the table, talking with Papa. Then he took from his pocket a hand-carved dreidel. He gave the top a twist, and it spun across the table, tipping and wobbling until it landed *gimel* side up.

"Take all. I have just made a lucky spin, and the game has not even started." He smiled and lifted his eyebrows at Adar, then grinned an invitation to me.

"We have nothing to gamble with," Adar said.

To our surprise, Isaac pulled a bag of acorns from his coat pocket and placed it on the table next to the dreidel. "I have been like a squirrel, saving for this," he said.

Ruth scampered over. "Will you let us play?"

Isaac nodded, and counted equal shares of the small round nuts for himself and Adar and Ruth and Papa and me. Isaac's younger daughter came and sat on his knee, and his older rested her chin on the table, high enough so she could see.

We played late into the night, watching the four-sided top balance and spin, the Hebrew letters changing with each roll. Papa spun shin too many times and finally had to give all his acorns to the center pile. He lost early and moved to the stove to read.

A little while later, Ruth and the little girls left the table one by one to curl up like balls of yarn on the bed. Isaac's pile of acorns grew larger and larger. Adar's and my own grew smaller.

Finally, when Adar had nothing left to gamble, Isaac took half of his winnings and pushed them over the table to her side. As he did this, he caught her hands in his. Adar blushed and glanced sideways at Papa, who was still reading. She smiled brightly and began playing again.

I wanted to play longer, too, but had no more acorns. Adar did not offer me any of hers, so I found a place on the bed next to Ruth and stretched out, watching the candles of the menorah burn.

I do not know when I fell asleep or at what hour Isaac left. I only remember Papa telling Isaac he thought another storm was coming.

"Too many storms," Isaac said. "One ends and another begins. The cow and horse are getting thin."

Papa sighed. "We have been trying to save enough money to buy hay for them."

"The weather teases us," Isaac said. "It clears up, enough to give us hope, then snows again."

"We will pray for an early spring."

"My knees are making dents in the floor."

I dreamed about Mazel. He was not in the pasture, but at our table, thin and hungry, watching the top spin. I had gambled my last acorns, the ones I needed to feed him.

It was my turn. I picked up the dreidel and spun it, watching it pirouette smoothly. Then it began to wobble, leaning first one way and then the other, slowly, more slowly, tipping, back and forth … back and …

The wind rattled our shutters and a cold draft slipped under our door, snuffing out the flames of our candles. I woke up, shivering, without knowing which way the dreidel had landed.

19

Adar is angry with me. She does not think I should go with Minnie to Cotopaxi without Papa's permission.

"It is to collect coal," I told her. "Look at how little we have left."

Adar put her hands on her hips and looked at the coal bucket next to the stove. Only a few pieces remained in the bottom, even though we have mixed it with wood to make it stretch.

"And what makes you so sure you can find some?"

"It is where the trains stop, and there are always a few pieces along the track."

"Hmmmmf." Adar looked at the coal bucket again. She took a dish from the soapy water in the dishpan and began to scrub. "You could get hurt," she said, "and then what will I tell Papa?"

"I will be with the others. Minnie and Etta and Sarah are going, and Mazel, too."

"Mazel!" Adar plunked the dish in the rinse pan and reached for another to wash. "If we sold that useless horse, we would have money enough for coal."

"He is not useless!" I cried. "He can help carry things, and we can ride him if we get tired."

"For sure now I know you are not going," she said. "What are you thinking, to be riding that horse?"

I could not rein my words in. "I have ridden Mazel many times. It is easy. I think even you could do it."

Adar dropped a plate into the dishpan and soapy water splashed up onto her face. She did not wipe it away, but glared at me through the suds. "It is not enough that we have lost little Leb. Now I must tell Papa you have fallen off a horse and broken your neck!"

I tried to find the words to calm her. "I am still in one piece," I said. "Mazel is a good horse. He does not buck or kick. I will teach you to ride, too, if you want."

Adar threw her arms in the air. "And then there will be two of us with a broken neck." She wiped her face with her sleeve and turned back to finish the dishes.

A minute later, she realized I was still standing there waiting for an answer. She waved her hand at me and said, "Go! Go! What do I care if I lose a sister?" When she said the word "sister," her voice quivered, then she collapsed into a chair with a moan and buried her head in her hands.

"I will stay if you like," I said quietly.

Adar waved me away again, and I tiptoed out. As I closed the door behind me, I heard Ruth say, "You still have me and Bella Rose." It was the name she had given to her doll.

"Perhaps Bella Rose can do Emma's chores if she gets hurt," Adar said.

As it turned out, it was not me who got hurt. On the way back up the mountain, Etta twisted her ankle on a loose stone. She crumpled to the ground and sat there rocking back and forth, moaning and holding her foot. I did not think we would ever get her home.

"Can you try to stand?" Minnie asked.

Etta made a whimpering sound, and with the help of Sarah and Minnie, struggled to her feet. When she tried to take a step, she fell again, folding in the middle like Ruth's doll.

"We must get you on the horse," Minnie said, helping her to stand once more.

A frightened look crossed Etta's face. She shook her head. "I will be all right in a minute."

Etta leaned on me for support and limped forward a few steps, wincing in pain. She would have fallen again, but Sarah caught her under the other arm. We hobbled a little farther up the trail like a three-headed cow.

After a few more steps, Etta stopped to catch her breath. She glanced up the long trail ahead of us, then back at Minnie, who held Mazel's reins.

"Mazel is a good horse," I said, rubbing my sore shoulder and thinking, *I will be as flat as a latke if I have to hold Etta up all the way home.*

"He will not throw me off?"

"No," I assured her.

"He will not run?"

"I will lead you," Minnie said. "And Emma and Sarah can walk next to you."

That is how we got Etta up the mountain. She would not straddle the horse, but sat sideways alongside the bag of coal, with both legs dangling. I kept one hand up to steady her legs, and Sarah walked opposite, holding Etta's backside.

"Have mercy!" Etta clutched Mazel's mane and mumbled the prayer for safe passage over and over again.

When we got home, Adar ran out to meet us. "What has happened?" she asked worriedly. "Why is Etta riding the horse?"

We told her about Etta's ankle, and she looked at me in horror. "It could have been you. It could have been you!" She repeated this over and over. Then she helped Etta down. "You must stay with us tonight."

Etta shook her head. "I think I am better." She limped a few steps, and although the foot was swollen she could put her full weight on it.

I tried to take Adar's attention away from Etta's foot. "Look at all the coal we have brought." I untied the bag. "And there will be more tomorrow, after the trains pass through."

"There will not be a tomorrow," Adar said, putting her hands on her hips. "Look what has happened to Etta."

"I am fine," Etta said. "And things would have been worse if we had not had our Mazel with us." Etta patted Mazel on the neck.

Adar shook her head. "What *mazel* is it to have a swollen ankle?" She looked at me. "What *mazel* is it to have a sister like you?" She went inside, taking a few chunks of coal with her.

The next morning our fire still had hot embers, and Adar agreed to let me go again. "I will probably be sorry for this," she said.

"I will be fine. You will see."

"You can only go if it does not snow again and the trail is clear." Adar paused. "And if Papa asks, it was not me who let you go."

"Papa will not find out."

A few weeks later, Papa was frowning when he came home. He washed his hands and face and sat down for the Sabbath prayers, studying me slowly before bowing his head. After we had eaten, he said, "How is it that a daughter of mine is picking coal from the track without my permission?"

I swallowed hard, trying to think how to answer, when Ruth blurted, "Papa, it is cold without the coal. Our fire goes dead in the night, and the water is frozen by morning."

Papa did not answer. We ate in silence. In the dim light, I could see the cracked and reddened skin of Papa's swollen fingers. His coat, in spite of Adar's mending, now had too many loose threads to count.

How did Papa find out? I did not think it was Adar who told him. Suddenly I remembered the train that was stopped at the water tower the last time we were in Cotopaxi.

The man sitting in the locomotive leaned out of the window and yelled to us, "Are you women from the Jewish colony?"

Minnie nodded and waved, bending to pick up a piece of coal. I walked behind her, leading Mazel with the empty bag tied to his back.

131

"We know your menfolk," the man hollered down. "We see them along the tracks hauling timbers. They are hard workers."

Minnie found another piece of coal and dropped it in the bag.

"Doesn't Mr. Black have coal at his store?" the man continued.

"We cannot afford to buy it."

The man turned around and yelled to someone behind him. Three black chunks flew from the coal car, landing near the track.

"Thank you," Minnie said. "May God bless you."

"May God bless you," the man replied. A hiss of steam muffled his words.

"Can you say hello to Jonas Solomon?" Minnie shouted up to him as the engine began to chug.

"Can you say hello to my papa?" I yelled.

"What is your name?" The engineer leaned out and twisted around to hear me.

"Emma." It was my first conversation in English. "Papa is tall. He wears a black *shtreimel*." I pointed to my head.

"Hat," Minnie said in English.

The train lurched forward, and the engineer waved back to us. When the caboose had passed, we crossed the tracks and found a few more chunks of coal that had been tossed beside the track. I did not think any more about it until I saw Papa's frown.

After we cleared the table, Papa walked to the stove to warm his hands. He sighed and looked over at me. "And the horse? You have been riding it, have you not?"

"Papa, Mazel is helping us. He carries the coal, and sometimes … when our feet are very tired …" I wondered if he had already heard the story of Etta and her sprained ankle.

Papa raised one eyebrow at me. "What would your mama be thinking right now?" he asked me.

I tried to bring Mama's face into my mind, but all I could see were the two pieces of the photo torn by the wheels of the train. "Minnie said that in America—"

"Minnie, Minnie, Minnie," Adar interrupted. "How did she get to be an expert on America? We should sell the horse and buy the coal we need."

"No! Mazel is *my* horse!" I shouted. Papa gave me such a stern look that I swallowed everything else I wanted to say.

Later, Papa asked me to come outside with him. I buttoned my coat and followed him up the starlit path to the pasture fence. There Papa stopped. He leaned on the top rail, shifting from foot to foot and breathing little white clouds of vapor into the icy air.

My heart filled with dread. I stood by Papa, waiting and listening to the hoofbeats pounding toward us in the dark. A moment later Mazel arrived, stretching his neck over the fence, wanting me to scratch him.

Finally, Papa spoke. "Ruth's shoes have cardboard in them to keep out the cold. All our earnings go to Mr. Black's store to pay off our debt and keep food on our table. There is little left."

I swallowed hard, stroking Mazel's mane. I did not want to listen to what Papa had to say.

"It's the horse," Papa said quietly. "Soon there will be no

more feed. It would be better, as Adar says, to sell him."

"Papa …" A lump grew in my throat. I stared at Mazel's bridle on the nearby post, and it blurred as I tried to blink away my tears. "Papa …"

"He is thin. You would not want to see him die of hunger." Papa paused. "I have been writing letters to Denver asking for help, but so far, there have been no answers. If there is no reply, a decision must be made."

I looked away from Papa and wiped my eyes. *Mazel, I thought, after all this I am going to lose you, too.*

Papa reached out and squeezed my shoulder, but it did not comfort me. "If there is no more snow, we can wait a little longer … a week … maybe two." He sighed. "But if the pasture is covered again …"

Papa did not finish his thought, but stood for a long moment staring at the dark outline of the Blood of Christ Mountains. He sighed again, turned slowly, and walked away back toward the house. His boots squeaked on the frozen ground.

20

I have learned some things about Colorado snow. There is snow that comes on little ghost feet, dusting the ground lightly before moving on. There is snow that comes in large flakes and melts away the next day when the sun shines. Then there is snow that comes with the bitter cold and stays and stays, stinging like little needles when it blows in your face. It never ends.

This morning, when we opened the door, a great drift of snow blocked our way. We brushed it away, but more kept falling.

"Why isn't Papa coming home?" Ruth asked.

"The tracks are closed, and the trains can't get through." Adar opened the door to the cookstove and poked at the coals. She added a stick of wood to the fire.

"Why can't they open them?"

"It is the snow and rock slides," I told her, wondering if the boy Charlie had made it safely back down the mountain after delivering the message to us. "It will probably be spring before we see him."

Adar slammed the firebox door and scowled at me.

Large tears welled up in Ruth's eyes. "I want to see Papa now."

I cracked the door to look outside, and a few minutes later cracked it again. Adar snapped at me. "Do something with yourself. You are turning me into a crazy person."

I wrapped my feet in flour sacks, put on two sweaters and my coat, and went out into the fresh snow, making tracks through the pasture gate. Mazel stood under a large pine tree where the branches made an umbrella above him. Snow melted off his back and rolled down his sides. Icicles hung from his underbelly.   ,

Nearby, I could see places in the snow where he had pawed the ground trying to find something to eat, and as I waded out to him, I wished I'd had something to bring him. I could feel the bones of his ribs when I stroked the white angel on his side.

"Papa will get answers to the letters soon," I told Mazel. "Then we can buy hay and oats for you to eat." I tried to believe this. I prayed and prayed it would be true.

A sheath of snow slid off a nearby branch and thundered to the ground beside us. Mazel was startled and galloped away. I stood for a moment, listening to the beat of my heart. Fear crept inside me like the frozen cold that slipped through the seams of my coat.

Papa, hurry home. I did not like to think about him being out in weather like this. I did not like to think of anyone being out in this cold. I pulled up the collar of my coat and hurried back to the house. My tracks were already gone.

21

What would Mama do? I have said those words over and over to myself and wished time and again that I had not listened to that voice inside me.

Adar says we are lucky. They could have killed us, or taken our milk cow, and then where would we be?

"If I had answered the door," Adar said, "I would not have let them in."

"They were cold," I said. "And the baby ..."

At first I did not see the baby, a lump on the woman's back underneath the blankets and furs. She looked like the crooked man I saw on the streets of New York, holding out a tin cup for money. As she stood there in our doorway, the hump on her back wiggled, not much, just a tiny bit. I had to look twice to make sure of what I saw.

Then I remembered her—the woman with the scar on her face. I remembered the tight deerskin dress that now hung limp, and I knew then that the bump on her back was a baby bundled in blankets.

I remembered, too, the Indian boy next to her—the boy I

had seen by the fire. His feet were wrapped in rabbit skins and tied with strips of leather.

"Food."

It sounded more like a grunt, and at first I did not understand him. Then he lifted his head slightly, holding one hand over his stomach, making sign language the way Minnie did when she was teaching me a new English word.

The door hung open for a long moment, letting in the freezing night air. I looked over my shoulder at Adar, stirring the pot of soup made by adding water to last night's mixture of onions, turnips, and carrots. Ruth sat on the bed, her eyes as round as the bowls on the table. A tiny voice inside my head asked, *What would Mama do?*

At that moment, I heard a little whimper from underneath the blankets on the woman's back. I made up my mind, waved them inside, and closed the door.

Adar dropped the serving spoon, splattering soup onto the hot stove top. She glared at me and backed away as the woman and boy walked toward the stove and held their hands above the heat.

The woman removed her blankets and lowered the baby from her back. It was in a little crib made from a flat board covered with leather that had been stitched with colored beads. When the woman pulled back the covering, I could see the baby's face, all wrinkly like a cabbage that had been left in the root cellar too long.

Ruth lost her shyness and scampered over. She stood on tiptoe and touched the baby's face, but the boy pushed her away and stood between them.

"No," he said, and this time I could understand him clearly.

The mother spoke to the boy in their own language, and he stepped back. She lowered the baby for Ruth to see, and she stepped forward, this time a little more timidly, and gently stroked the baby's black hair.

"The soup is getting cold." Adar dropped the ladle into the empty pot and placed two more bowls on our table. We had bread left over from our noon meal and a small portion of cheese we had been saving from the round Papa had brought home weeks earlier.

The boy took his soup and sat down on the floor, leaning his back against the wall and tipping the bowl with both hands to drink it instead of using a spoon. The woman leaned the flat board with the baby in it next to him, got her soup, and gulped it hurriedly.

The bread, too, they tore apart and devoured, not even waiting for Adar to finish our prayers. Adar prayed loudly, pointing her words like sharp knives at our guests. When she finished, we ate in silence, sipping slowly to make each spoonful last. About halfway through my soup, I noticed the boy standing next to me, his bowl empty.

"We have no more." Adar tipped the empty pot toward him and banged the inside with the ladle.

The boy looked at the soup in my bowl and the small piece of bread on my plate. It made me think about Mazel, thin and hungry, outside in the cold, and I felt sorry for him. I poured what was left of my soup into his bowl and handed him my bread.

Adar dropped the empty pot onto the table and sat down, throwing up her arms. "So starve if you want to."

I tried not to think about it, but later I could not sleep for the ache in my stomach. In the middle of the night, I heard the baby whimper and the rustling sound as the mother brought it close to her. It was the baby's suckling that put me to sleep. I dreamed of Mama and little Leb.

In the morning, when I woke up, the Indians were gone. I could not believe it, but worse, I could not believe what I saw when I went to the creek for water. The snow had stopped falling, and I easily found tracks, turning toward the horse pasture.

I put down my buckets and followed them to the pasture gate. There I stopped. The gate was open, and Mazel's bridle was gone.

"Mazel!" I shouted.

Hoofprints and footprints came through the pasture gate. For a short distance, two pairs of people tracks crisscrossed with Mazel's, then only one pair—the tracks of the boy's rabbit-skin-covered feet.

Finally, only Mazel's tracks remained, going down and away in the endless white snow.

"Mazel ..."

I ran, following the tracks until they joined the main trail, and still I ran, searching for any sign of them.

Finally I reached the bush that held the tattered pieces of

Papa's white handkerchief and fell to my knees in the snow. The frayed strands of the shredded cloth drooped like frozen fingers pointing; to the last trace of my good-luck horse.

$$22$$

"I see Papa coming! He is home." Ruth had just finished bringing in firewood for the evening. She dropped it and ran back outside.

"Oh, hurry," Adar said. "Help me tidy up." She stood wiping her hands on her apron and looking around the room.

I looked, too, wondering what could be left to tidy. Every day since Papa had left, we had tidied—the shelves, the pots and pans, the bed, the floor, the walls, the ceiling, and we'd even dusted the pages of Papa's Bible.

Adar smoothed our tablecloth and placed the Sabbath candle in the center, looking around again. "There is no challah. What will Papa say?"

I peeked out the door to see Ruth walking up to the house, holding Papa's hand. "Did the rocks get cleared from the tracks? Did you have to lift them off yourself?"

Papa entered the house and dropped his bundle. He picked Ruth up and cradled her in his arms, giving her a big kiss before putting her down.

Adar stood quietly on the other side of the table. "You are

here just in time. God has blessed us, but"—she lowered her eyes—"our flour is gone, and I could not make bread."

Papa pulled a small bag from his bundle and placed it in Adar's hands. "In a few days there will be more. We have news from Denver." He took a letter from his coat pocket and waved it at us. "They have sent money to help pay our debt at Mr. Black's store, and when the weather is better, they will send us shoes and clothing."

Adar threw her arms around him, and he hugged her back tightly. "Papa, we're going to make it until spring!"

Papa looked over at me. "I have some news for you, too. There is hay coming … enough for both the cow and the horse."

I dropped onto the bed and burst into tears, pressing my hands to my face. I sobbed, "Papa, Mazel is gone. There is no horse left to feed."

Slowly Papa walked over and sat down beside me on the bed. Too old to fit onto his lap like Ruth, and too young to be hugged in a grown-up way like Adar, I sat stiffly like our iron bed frame, too miserable to move.

"It was the Indians," Ruth blurted. "They came here and stole our horse."

Adar tried to shush her, but already Ruth was running away with the story of the boy and the woman and the baby and how they stayed with us and left before daylight and took the horse and rode away without even saying thank you or good-bye.

"Emma let them in," Adar said, finishing the story and folding her arms over her chest. "Otherwise, they would have

143

just gone away. She has the brains of a potato."

Papa was silent for a long moment, looking from Ruth to Adar and then settling his gaze on me. I did not look at him, but stared down at my hands where they had fallen cold and limp into my lap.

"Emma," Papa said gently. "Can you look at me?"

I already knew what he would say. He would tell me how the Indians could have stolen Ruth or me or all of us. He would tell me that I had made a terrible mistake, and next time I should think first before I act. Papa would agree with Adar that I have the brains of a potato.

I could not look at Papa, but stared and stared at my hands, and I would be sitting there still, but Ruth told me I was squishing Bella Rose. I stroked the horse hair on Bella Rose's head and handed her to Ruth, remembering the way Mazel felt when I petted him.

"Maybe Mazel will come back," Ruth said.

Maybe he will, I hoped.

Every day, I walked to the pasture gate looking for his tracks. I walked around the fence and down the trail to the place where Papa's handkerchief hung.

At first, my shoes slipped on the snow-packed trail, and then the trail turned to slush so that when I returned home Adar scolded me for getting my feet wet. Finally the trail turned to mud with little rivulets of water running down it from the melting snow.

One day, after most of the snow had melted, I saw horse tracks coming up the main trail to the houses. My feet could

144

not hurry fast enough to follow them. When I got to our house, I discovered it was only Mr. Black bringing something for Papa.

"'March,'" Minnie told me one morning when it was warm enough to sit outside for our English lessons, "is the word for the month we are in."

"And what will come next?" Ruth asked.

"April," Minnie said.

We heard a rumbling sound and then two wagons appeared, making their way up the mountain trail. The boy Charlie from the hotel waved at us.

"Some supplies are here for you," he called, "all the way from Denver."

People came from their houses to help unload boxes of shoes and dresses and pants and shirts of all colors. Next to them large sacks of oats and barley, beans, and tins of meat were arranged in rows so everyone would have a chance to take some.

"It is like market day in Kishinev," Ruth said excitedly.

"I am sorry we could not get here sooner," the wagon driver said in Yiddish, and it surprised me to hear a visitor who was not speaking English. "The snow was too much, even in Denver. At last it looks like winter is gone."

I looked around at the patches of remaining white near the sides of the houses and in the shade of the bushes and trees. The wagons had carved deep ruts in the ground with their wheels.

"You are just in time," Papa said. "If you had come sooner, the road would have been too slippery. Because of the thaw, we cannot work, and we are able to be here to welcome you."

"Would you like a candy?" I turned to see the boy Charlie standing next to his horse.

My heart leapt. The horse was brown, like Mazel, with white on his face! Then I looked again. The white did not have the same star shape, and this horse had no white on its side. I took the peppermint stick and broke off a piece to eat. I broke off a second piece and held it out for the horse, thinking of Mazel and how he used to nuzzle me for treats.

"Does your horse have a name?" I said in my best English, and realized the boy had spoken to me in English first, and I had understood him.

"It is Star," he said. "He belongs to Mr. Black. He's a brother to the horse you have."

Minnie stood nearby and translated for me when I needed help. I asked her how he knew about Mazel.

"Everyone knows," Minnie said. "In Mr. Black's store they call you the crazy girl that saved the horse."

I did not like being called the crazy girl and was going to say so when Charlie said, "I wish Mr. Black had not sold him to that traveler. He was my favorite horse. Can I see him?"

Minnie hesitated before translating for me. When she did, the sweet peppermint taste in my mouth turned bitter. I looked away.

Just then, Adar waved me over to a pile of dresses. "Come see if you can find something that will fit." She held a dress up to Ruth, eyeing it for size, then she said to the wagon driver, "If you would like to take our old dresses back to Denver, you may."

The man took one look at Ruth's raggedy clothes and shook his head. The sleeves of her dress had worked their way up her arms, and the skirt had been patched so many times it looked like a rag quilt.

"Try this one," Adar said to Ruth. "And one for you." She handed me a dark blue dress with a high collar and long sleeves. Then she began to rummage again, holding each dress up for inspection. "Too big. Too small." She frowned. "There must be more somewhere."

I looked down the row of boxes and saw Isaac Kessel holding up a dress, inspecting it. When he saw me watching him, he dropped it quickly, and his face turned a bright red.

Adar continued to rummage. "Nothing is right." She placed her hands on her hips.

Down the row, Mr. Kessel picked up the dress again and walked over, slipping it into Adar's hands sideways without looking at her.

Adar took the dress and held it up. She burst into a radiant smile, hugging the dress and skipping a little. Isaac stared at his feet in embarrassment, but I could see the ends of his mustache twitch.

"Look at the shoes I have found!" Ruth called. She put them on and skittered over.

"I think now we can all go dancing," Papa said, pulling on a pair of boots that fit him.

Isaac Kessel, still standing near Adar, clicked his heels in the air and landed in a deep bow at Adar's side. Her face turned scarlet, but she laughed, and I had to look twice to make sure

147

my ears and eyes were not playing tricks on me.

The empty wagons started back down the hill, with Charlie leading the way. As I watched them go, a brown bird with a fat red chest landed in a puddle of melted snow. It fluttered its wings, giving itself a quick bath, then flew to a low branch on a nearby bush, whistling a beautiful song.

"It is a robin," Minnie told me, using the English word. "It is the bird of spring."

Everyone is happy but me, I thought. *Ruth has new shoes. Adar has a nice dress. The milk cow has food to eat, and the chickens have made little nests for a new brood of chicks. If only Mazel were here to eat the sprigs of tender green grass that are pushing up through the moist soil.*

Minnie must have known what I was thinking. She said, "Maybe we can get another horse."

I know she was trying to make me feel better, but I did not want another horse. I wanted my Mazel.

23

If Mama were here, she would find a way to make the job of the Passover cleaning a happy time. Instead, Adar is a slave driver, using her tongue as a whip to order Ruth and me around.

"Scrub harder," she tells Ruth, whose little hands are frozen from the cold creek water.

"My hands are numb," Ruth says miserably.

"It is too early in the day to light the stove, and we must save our wood for the Pesach baking."

Not to mention it was the stove we were working on, polishing every blackened plate and scrubbing the pipe until all the soot from the winter smoke disappeared.

"Bring me a small twig," Adar said, and Ruth scampered out, happy to be away from the house for a few moments. When she returned, Adar broke the twig into short pieces, dipped the end of one into our scrub water, and used it to dig the grime out of the grooves of the stove trim.

"You can help, too," she said when she noticed I was staring at her.

The three of us leaned over the stove like old ladies with bad eyesight. We used the twigs to trace the curved pattern of the skirting until the black in the creases disappeared and the stove glimmered.

Ruth put down her twig and made faces in the shiny metal, twisting sideways and scrunching up her nose, amused by her reflection. I tried a face, too, remembering the long, tall mirror at Mama's dressing table where she brushed our hair.

"And now for my day's work," Mama used to say when it was my turn.

Ruth's thin, straight hair took only a few minutes to comb, and Adar kept hers wrapped on her head so it stayed untangled. Not mine. Thick and unruly, it would not tame.

"Your hair would hold a nest of mice," Mama laughed as she brushed.

"Why can't I have hair like Adar's or Ruth's?" I asked her.

"Because you are not Adar or Ruth," Mama said. "You are you, and that is the way it is meant to be."

"It is sometimes hard to be me," I told Mama. Papa had just scolded me for leaving the gate to the chicken yard unlatched.

Mama made a twist in a strand of hair before braiding it. "Someday you will understand how special you are," she said.

My thoughts of Mama flew out the door with the scrub water. "Emma! We need the buckets filled, and when you get back, we will start on the walls."

And so we did the walls, and the floor, and the table and chairs and the bed frame, and then the undersides of the table and chairs and the bed frame. If we could have turned the floorboards upside down, we would have done the undersides of them, too.

"I do not know why they call this the 'festival of freedom,'" Ruth complained. "It is the festival of work!"

"Think of the potato kugel we will eat," Adar said.

"And carrot tzimmes." My mouth watered.

"Chicken stew with egg noodles," Adar added.

"Dumplings and potatoes."

Ruth brightened a little. "Why aren't we having the service in the synagogue?"

"It is easier to bake and prepare our food here," Adar said. "We are going to start on the matzo as soon as Papa comes back with the flour."

"We already have flour from Mr. Black's store," Ruth pointed out.

"Papa is buying special Passover flour," Adar explained. "The kosher flour. He is walking all the way to Salida to get it."

We had been so busy cleaning, I had not even missed Papa. "He will be home tomorrow in the afternoon," I added.

"By that time we will have the blankets and mattresses washed, the lamp chimneys scrubbed, and the candlesticks polished." Adar scanned the room to make sure she had not forgotten anything. "Tonight we can do all the plates and silverware."

Ruth groaned. I picked up the buckets to fill them again, walking slowly past the turnoff to the horse pasture. My feet wanted to go there—to follow the trail to the pasture gate and look for Mazel, but I knew it would be empty. I kept on the trail to the creek and returned as Adar and Ruth were discussing the seder plans.

"The service will be in the clearing below the garden," Adar said, "instead of the synagogue. It's warm enough now. We'll carry our tables and chairs outside, where there is plenty of space."

"Will the others come?" Ruth asked about the people that lived in the houses below.

"Everyone," Adar said. "We will all be here together."

Not everyone, I thought. *Mama and little Leb will not be here. And Mazel. He will not be here either.*

24

My stomach is twisting in knots. Papa is not back. We kept the lamp lit for him most of last night. Finally Adar said we should turn it off so we would not waste the kerosene. Still, I could not sleep.

It is almost noon, and Papa is not here. I have been watching the trail all morning for his black hat, but all I see are crows flying up, caw-cawing, and landing again. Adar is beside herself, wringing her hands about how the bread will not get finished, but I think she is worried about Papa.

"There will be time to bake tomorrow," I told her. "And we have flour from Mr. Black's store."

"Why do you think Papa walked to Salida?" Adar snapped at me. "The Passover flour is from the Jewish grocer, and it has been ordered special."

"I will go look for him," I said. "Maybe he stopped for a rest at the lower houses."

"You will get lost again, and then who will I send to look for you?" She scolded me as though I were a small child, but a little line of worry wrinkled her brow, and I could tell she was thinking about it.

"I know the way now," I pressed. "I have been on the trail more times than you have."

Adar tucked a strand of hair behind her ear, put her hands on her hips, and sighed. She studied me, one piece at a time, from the top of my head down to the toes of my shoes. Then she walked to the window and looked out. The day, which had started out sunny, now had shadows of gray from gathering clouds.

Just then, the wind grabbed our door and slammed it. Adar opened it again and looked out. "You must wear your coat," she said. "And take something to eat."

"I will not need it—" I started to argue, then thought better of it and put on my coat before Adar changed her mind. I grabbed some bread to eat if I got hungry.

"Don't stop to talk." Adar followed me to the door. "If he is not there, come right back."

I hurried out, hoping I would meet Papa along the trail, but all I saw were little gray birds flickering in the trees and bushes. When I reached the lower houses, I went from one to the next, asking about Papa.

"We saw him when he passed through," Joseph Washer told me.

"No," Rivka said. "He promised to leave some flour when he came back."

"No, we have not seen him."

I decided it would not hurt to go a little farther and wait for Papa at the junction in Oak Grove Creek where the road turned west toward Salida. I would meet Papa there and help him carry the flour, the two of us, bringing it home just in time to make the matzo.

I made my way down the ridge to the creek. No Papa. A set of wagon tracks went down the creek, toward Cotopaxi, and a second set traveled west toward the mountains.

I tore off a small piece of bread to eat and returned the rest to my coat pocket. I could no longer see the mountains, which were shrouded in clouds. A cold wind bit my cheeks.

It is too cold to just stand here, I thought. My feet began to move one step, then two, along the road to Salida, patting out *Papa, Papa, Papa, Papa …*

I did not, at first, notice the single snowflakes that began to whirl and spin downward, melting as they touched the road, but then a blast of wind from the mountains brought with it a flurry of flakes that thickened and filled the shallow tracks made by wagon wheels.

I stopped, and shouted, "Papa!" The snowflakes multiplied, and now I could see only a few feet in front of me.

I buttoned my top button and turned up the collar of my coat. I looked behind me, and where my footprints had been, there was nothing but white.

I wondered how far I had come and how much longer it would be before sunset. With each step I became more anxious. Pine trees lined the road, enclosing me in a long, dark corridor … the Tsar's soldiers, looming above me in starched uniforms with foreboding black hats. They leered at me with twisted ghoulish faces. *You are lost … lost … lost.*

155

The wind stopped, and the snow no longer blew sideways but fell straight down. "Papa!" I shouted again. I strained my ears for an answer, but heard only the floating and landing of snowflakes.

Then I smelled smoke. At first I thought I was imagining it, but as I took a few more steps, the scent of the fire grew stronger. It could not be far. If I could get there, I would find people who would help me. Maybe it would be Papa, waiting out the storm.

I left the road at the place where the smoke smelled the strongest and tramped through the woods. I ducked below snow-covered branches and picked my way over deadfall, following the smell. The wet snow soaked through my shoes and slid down underneath my collar.

I could still smell the smoke, but it did not seem much closer.

"Papa, where are you?" I walked a few more steps and looked down. There on the ground were my own tracks, rapidly filling with snow.

I leaned against the wide trunk of a tree, staring through my tears at a blur of swirling flakes. How would I find my way back to the road? I did not care. I would lean against the tree until I grew roots, and later, after the storm, when Adar and Ruth came to look for me, I would have little green branches growing from my arms and leaves uncurling from my fingers.

As I thought these things, I heard a faint rustling sound. Something was in the woods not far from me. I wiped away my tears and peered through the falling snow. A dark shape shifted and moved toward me. Then an angel appeared with light fluttering wings.

A twig snapped. *Thump-thump*. The dark shape emerged no farther from me than I could throw a stone.

It was Mazel, my beautiful Mazel! I ran to him and threw my arms around his neck. "Mazel, you have found me! Like an angel from heaven you have come!"

He nuzzled my shoulder and made a small hop. *Thump*. I looked down and saw his feet were hobbled with two thick strands of braided leather. He could move only a few inches at a time in short little jumps.

I knew, then, whose fire it was: the woman and the boy who had eaten our food and stolen my Mazel. I trembled. Who else would be at the fire with them? I thought of the naked men with the knives.

The smell of smoke grew strong again. I could see Mazel's tracks between the trees, leading toward the smell. I cupped my frozen fingers inside the sleeves of my coat, trying to decide what to do. Maybe Mazel had been traded for money or food. Maybe it was someone else who owned him now.

My frozen toes and fingers made up my mind. I followed Mazel's tracks, thinking I would peek first to see who the fire belonged to.

A few feet from the camp, I stopped. I could hear the fire crackling and the voice of a man speaking. Next, a woman's voice barked a command, and footsteps came toward me.

I hid in the shadow of a tree, holding my breath. The Indian boy, whose face I will never forget, came so close to me I could almost reach out and touch his black braids. He picked up some wood and returned to the fire without noticing me.

I let out my breath and backed away, step by step. I would go back and wait with Mazel until my bones turned to frozen stones and my blood turned to ice. I would die before I went into that camp.

Then I noticed Mazel's bridle hanging on a low branch across from where I stood. To get it, I would have to stretch across the gap between the trees where I might be seen.

I hesitated, then stepped forward and reached for it, glancing sideways at the huddled group around the fire. Carefully I lifted the bridle from the branch, backed away, and turned. I ran without looking back, retracing my path in the snow.

When I reached Mazel, I slipped the bridle on and knelt down, working the hobbles off his feet with my stiff, frozen fingers. The leather loosened and one foot was free. The second only needed lifting from the loop. I finished and stood up, turning to face the fierce black eyes of the Indian boy.

I did not move.

The boy did not move.

We stood staring at each other until the snow slowed, and I could count the single flakes as they melted on the boy's head.

"My horse," I finally said in English, pointing first to myself and then to Mazel.

The boy's eyes darted sideways at Mazel and back again. "My horse." He thumped his chest with a closed fist.

"He is mine," I said in Yiddish, the pitch of my voice rising.

The boy's expression changed, and a look of recognition flickered in his eyes. He glanced over his shoulder in the direction of the camp. I heard a voice calling him, the same voice I had heard earlier, the voice of the woman.

Slowly, I pulled Mazel toward me, afraid the boy would call for his people, afraid he would try to stop me. I measured the distance from the ground to Mazel's back, wondering if I could throw myself on him and ride him away.

The boy did not move or call out. Instead, he spoke slowly to me in English. "Food," he said. "You give food."

I blinked at him, remembering the soup and bread. His eyes seemed to soften, and I knew then he would not stop me, that he would let me take my Mazel back home.

I walked Mazel to a nearby stump, where I could get high enough to swing my leg up over him. As I did, I heard the woman calling again. Without looking back, I flung myself up on Mazel, kicked hard, and pressed myself low to his neck, praying we would be able to find our way out of the forest and back to the road.

We plunged under snow-covered branches and wove between tall ponderosas and thick undergrowth until we came to a break in the trees. I slowed Mazel, and we stepped into the light of the long corridor that was the road to Salida. Above the trees, a patch of clear sky showed between the clouds.

It is Papa's *shtreimel* I remember the most as he approached. It reminded me of the duck we saw bobbing on the water when our boat came into New York Harbor. At first you could see only a dark spot on the horizon, then a wave would roll up, and

159

the spot would disappear, then reappear again, only this time closer, until finally you could make out the shape of a duck's head and neck and body.

After the hat, I recognized Papa's tattered black coat, then the graying tasseled fringe of his beard. Finally I could see light reflected off Papa's glasses as the sun peeked out between patches of the fast-moving clouds.

"Papa!" I shouted. I waved from Mazel's back and trotted toward him, slowing and sliding to the ground next to him. "Papa!" I flung myself at him and cried, burying my face in his coat.

"Emma, Emma. What has happened? Why are you here?" Papa put down his bundle and stroked my hair until I stopped crying.

The world seemed suddenly still. I lifted my head and looked at the sky, where a few remaining clouds in the west billowed and blended into a peach-and-melon-colored sunset. Below, the earth was frosted as white and pure as the Passover flour.

"How did you come here?" Papa finally asked. "And where did you find Mazel?"

I started to tell him, then looked down at his foot, noticing his rolled-up pants leg and loosely laced boot. Inside the boot, he had wrapped strips of cloth around and around to make a sturdy brace. "Papa, you are hurt."

"It is not bad," he said, "but I'm afraid it has slowed me down."

"You must ride Mazel," I said.

160

He would not, but agreed to tie the bundle that held the Passover flour to Mazel's back, and we walked down the road together, making prints in the freshly fallen snow.

As we walked, I told Papa my story. He said very little until the light faded, and we stopped at the side of the road to make a camp. He built a fire, and we pulled branches from a nearby cedar tree to make a dry place to sit. I shared the bread from my coat pocket with him.

When that was done, Papa tucked me underneath the wing of his coat and spread his blanket across our knees. As I stared sleepily at the flames of the fire, he said, "Of all my daughters, you are the most like your mother. You are very special to me."

"I am like Mama?" I could not believe this was true.

He nodded.

When I lay my head back on his chest, I felt a hard lump. "Papa, there is something bumpy in your pocket."

Papa reached in and brought out the velvet cloth that held Mama's ring. He unwrapped it slowly and said, "I've been meaning to give this to you."

"But, Papa—"

"Shhhhh." Papa put the ring back into the cloth and pressed it into my hand. He squeezed my fingers gently, the way he used to squeeze Mama's when she was alive.

The velvet cloth warmed my hand. I curled it up next to my heart, holding it tightly. My eyelids closed.

25

It is Adar I see first running down the trail to Oak Grove Creek. She is followed by Ruth and Minnie and Etta … too many to count. They are flying off the hill one at a time, a flutter of skirts and scarves and coats and hats against a background of rocks, sand, and melting snow.

"What a blessing this is! I can't believe my eyes," Sarah says. "We have been up searching since daybreak."

Papa sits atop Mazel, balancing the large bundle of flour on his lap. He had agreed to ride only after I convinced him how much quicker it would be.

Adar just glances at him, then scolds me. "You think it is better to have the whole world lost? I have walked holes in our floor, worrying about you."

Then Ruth runs up to me, breathless, and grabs my hand. "Emma, I thought the bears had eaten you!"

"Foolish girl," Etta says, shaking her head. "We have not slept all night for worry." And then she grabs me and holds me so tightly I think I will break into pieces.

"Papa is here, too," I say, embarrassed by all the attention.

The conversation stops for a moment as eyes turn to Papa sitting on Mazel's back.

"And did I not say he would be here in time to make the matzos?" Sarah acts as if his appearance is nothing unusual, but mine is a miracle from the angels.

"And the horse!" Ruth exclaims. "Papa has brought back Mazel."

"I have not brought back the horse," Papa says, pointing to his injured foot. "Emma's horse has brought back me."

"Emma's horse." The words warm me like the sunlight melting the sparkling snow.

Then Adar does a surprising thing. She grabs Mazel's cheeks with both hands and gives him a kiss, not a little peck, but a large, sloppy kiss on his rubbery lips. Mazel wrinkles his nose, showing his teeth, and sneezes.

"I think you should be careful," Etta says to Adar. "The matchmaker might be getting an idea or two."

Everyone laughs as Adar blushes and looks over her shoulder at Isaac Kessel. He smiles at her.

I am on the mountainside on the flat below the garden wall. We are all here: Minnie, Rachel, Rivka, Etta, Sarah, Helen, Reva, Assna, Benjamin, Saul, Isaac, Abraham, Joseph, Jonas, Shem, Ezra …

Every one of us … and of course, Papa and Adar and Ruth.

Our prayers and stories are ended, and I am so full of food I cannot think of eating one more bite, unless it is to have a tiny bit more of Etta's sweet potato pudding that melts in your mouth.

The light is fading, and Papa is chanting. His voice drifts on the warm spring breeze. I watch the full moon rise and the first stars flicker in the ebony sky.

Suddenly I catch my breath. A single star appears on the horizon and shines more brightly than the others. A warm glow fills my heart, and I know in an instant it is Mama, looking down at me from above.

A moment later, a smaller star appears. It winks at me, and I hear a little voice saying "Hohshy."

"Horsey," I whisper back, and blow a kiss to Leb.

At that moment a single coyote starts a long lament that echoes up into the ridges of the mountains and out across the valley floor. A second coyote adds its howl, and another, and another, and another.

I look up at the star-filled sky, then gaze around me at my people. For the first time since arriving in America, I am not alone.

Author's Note

W hile Emma's story is a work of fiction, there is much truth in it. On May 8, 1882, a group of Russian Jewish immigrants arrived in Cotopaxi, Colorado, to form an agricultural colony. They were promised housing and rich ground for farming. Instead, the land they received was rocky and of poor quality, which made growing crops difficult. The houses were not what they had been led to expect, either. They were small and unfinished, and the colonists lacked equipment and livestock for tilling and planting.

The original Jewish settlers faced many of the same hardships that Emma and her family did. There was an early frost, and the crops were stunted. The colonists were also threatened by marauding bears and visited in the winter by starving Indians, who came to their doors begging for food.

The unusually harsh winter of 1882 left the colonists broke and starving. They took jobs in a local mine for $1.50 a day, $2.50 if they worked at night. They also worked for the railroad, sawing and hauling logs of one foot or more in diameter. Two or three men would balance the enormous logs on their shoulders and carry them down steep slopes to the track. They were paid a penny per log. If it had not been for the help they received from the Jewish community in Denver, the colonists would not have made it through that first winter.

The colonists set out to own their own land, and stories and records show that they traveled to Canon City by wagon in the fall of 1882 to fill out the papers to do this. The declarations turned out to be nothing more than statements of occupancy with no legal rights of ownership.

On the brighter side, the first summer for the Jewish immigrants held the joy of establishing a synagogue in Cotopaxi. A great celebration followed the dedication of the Sefer Torah, where, according to Allen duPont Breck in his book *The Centennial History of the Jews of Colorado, 1859-1959*, "the silent moon sent its silvery rays upon the dancing and singing Russians." The Torah (sacred religious scroll) was donated to them and came all the way from New York. Two marriages were performed in the new synagogue.

At the end of the first summer, the colony numbered sixty-three. Two babies and one child died at Cotopaxi, and there were several new births. By the spring of 1883, however, many of the colonists decided to leave, and by 1884, the colony was dissolved.

After that, many of the people from the Cotopaxi Colony moved to Denver, where they became leaders in the Jewish community. Others became successful farmers in different parts of Colorado and other states where the climate and soil were more suitable for agriculture.

Even though the colony itself was not a success, the resilience and sheer heart of the people continue to echo in the mountains, valleys, and plains of Colorado. The colonists' bravery, and the bravery of many like them, has helped to build our nation.

Acknowledgments

I wish to thank the following people for help in writing this book: Charme Krauth and her father, Richard Milstein, for visits and conversations about their family history; Linda Kramer for careful reading; LaQuita Dunn for help with research; and my husband, Steve, for providing me with a cushion of love and support.

A special thanks to Doris and Tom Baker of Filter Press for believing in this book and making it a part of their publishing program that promotes the love of Colorado History through fiction and nonfiction books.

About the Author

Nancy Oswald is an author, speaker, and retired elementary teacher. She writes middle grade and young adult historical fiction.

Since the publication of the hardcover edition of *Nothing Here but Stones* in 2004, Nancy has authored *Hard Face Moon* (Filter Press, 2008) and *Rescue in Poverty Gulch* (Filter Press, 2011). All three books are works of historical fiction set in the early days of Colorado.

Nothing Here but Stones received the WILLA Literary Award from Women Writing the West in 2005.

Nancy lives on a working cattle ranch in the Sangre de Cristo Mountains of Colorado. Contact her for presentations, school visits, and signings through her website *www.NancyOswald.com* or by emailing *authors@ FilterPressBooks.com.*